SEVENTEEN TOMATOES

Seventeen Tomatoes

~

TALES FROM KASHMIR

Jaspreet Singh

ESPLANADE
Books

THE FICTION SERIES AT VÉHICULE PRESS

Published with the generous assistance of The Canada Council for the Arts, the Book Publishing Industry Development Program of the Department of Canadian Heritage. and the Société de développement des entreprises culturelles du Québec (SODEC).

The excerpts on page 52 and 69 are from the poem "The Last Saffron," and the excerpt on page 63 is from the poem "After the August Wedding in Lahore," both from *The Country Without a Post Office* by Agha Shahid Ali (W.W. Norton). The excerpt from the poem "The Seasons of the Plains" (page 60) is from *The Half-Inch Himalayas* by Agha Shahid Ali (Wesleyan University Press). The excerpt from the poem "Rebirth" (page 82) is from *A Lonely Woman: Forugh Farrokhzad and Her Poetry* by Michael C. Hillman (Mage Publishers).

Esplanade Books editor: Andrew Steinmetz
Cover design: David Drummond
Author photo (p. 159): Terence Byrnes
Set in Minion by Simon Garamond
Printed by AGMV-Marquis Inc.

LIBRARY AND ARCHIVES CANADA CATALOGUING IN PUBLICATION
Singh, Jaspreet, 1969-
Seventeen tomatoes : tales from Kashmir / Jaspreet Singh.

Short stories.
ISBN 1-55065-188-9

I. Title.

PS8637.I53S48 2004   C813'.6   NA 30426721   C2004-904018-9

Published by Véhicule Press, Montréal, Québec, Canada
www.vehiculepress.com

Distribution in Canada by LitDistCo
orders@lpg.ca

Printed and bound in Canada.

For my parents,
who introduced me to Gardens.

Also, for Dilreen and Tanya–
marvellous gardeners.

Contents

Kashmir was like the face of the beloved that one sees in a dream and that fades away on wakening.

–Jawaharlal Nehru

~

Angle of Heaven

A little boy named Adi accompanied his father to an army camp on top of a glacier. His father, a tall Sikh, introduced him to men in red helmets.

"They are Engineers," he said.

The men were standing on the edge of a deep crevasse and looked busy, their hands gesticulating. The mercury was forty below. The light was faint, and the wind was strong.

"Don't be afraid," said the father, "ask them your question."

Adi couldn't think of a word. He inhaled, and then exhaled, a little bit longer. The vapor floated away from him just like incense in a monastery. There was no monastery around, only lumps of ice. He bent low and picked up ice.

"Sir," he began softly. "Sirs, what do you do in your free time?"

"Boy," answered an Engineer, "we compute the *Angle Of Heaven*."

"Is that all?" asked Adi, compressing the lump of ice in his fist.

"No, no. We were the first to estimate the number of mosques and temples and churches in Paradise. Our current project is to determine the chemical composition of Djinns."

"Details," added the man in the biggest helmet, "can be found in my treatise: *Mechanics of Doomsday and Life after Death*."

Those words overwhelmed Adi. Light but dense, clear but unclear—they were like the lump in his fist.

"So painful," he thought, "it almost gives me pleasure."

The ice stabbed him for a long time, before giving birth to drops, which escaped his warm fingers.

~

Seventeen Tomatoes

Adi and Arjun, fast friends, studied in the Model Boys' School in Kashmir. Classes were held in tents. Not far from the grade-three tent the boys could see a brick-and-cement building under construction. Mrs. Nargis, the teacher, told them that the construction was moving so slowly the building would be ready for the education of the boys' grandchildren.

The math class had just begun when a man in camouflage uniform entered the tent. A girl with half-closed eyes marched behind him carrying a school bag and seventeen tomatoes. She had a long ponytail and wore a dark blue pheran somewhat large for her.

"Where can my daughter sit?" asked the man loudly.

"She cannot sit," said Mrs. Nargis. "This is a boys' school."

The girl hid behind the man's back.

"Don't be afraid, girl," said the man. "Go sit anywhere."

Then he marched toward the teacher and loaded his revolver.

"Rules," said Mrs. Nargis, gasping for breath, "cannot be broken."

"There are no girls' schools in this area, Madam," he said. "Listen carefully: If you send my child home, I will shoot you."

The entire class hummed with fear and excitement.

"Silence!" Mrs. Nargis put her finger over her lips. "Pin-drop silence!"

Adi and Arjun wondered why the teacher didn't whip out her cane at that moment. Any trouble they made was always met with such a warning.

The military man scanned the tent with red eyes. The left side of the tent was full of boys; the right side of the tent was full of boys.

"Girl," said Mrs. Nargis, dead as a brick, "take my chair and sit in the middle."

Satisfied, the man unloaded the revolver and marched out toward the distant mountains. For a long time afterward the class could hear the echo of his footsteps pounding the path that led from the tent.

That day, Mrs. Nargis declared an early recess. During recess the girl stayed glued to her chair and began eating tomatoes. Adi and Arjun hesitantly inched toward her, as did the rest of the class. She was as still as a pebble, except for the movement caused by her eating. The boys told her their names; she nervously swallowed. The girl finished the sixth tomato faster than the fifth. When Arjun told her his name, she giggled with a sparkle in her eyes.

No one asked the girl her name. They also avoided the topic of her father. Instead, they bragged about the cities they had visited or the cricket matches they had won or the Amitabh-Rekha movies they had watched. They gave her strands of saffron. And Adi and Arjun promised her more gifts the next day: butterflies and answers to Mrs. Nargis's exams.

The girl didn't join them for football, but she watched them competing in the schoolyard through the tent window. She looked frightened, but continued eating the tomatoes, reddish-green fruits the size of Ping-Pong balls.

Adi and Arjun did not join the other boys in the yard. They

were rolling a bicycle tire inside the unfinished building. When the tire wobbled over a mound of cement, Arjun turned to his friend and confessed: "When I grow up I will marry her."

"Who?" Adi asked.

"The girl!"

"Then her father will shoot you," said Adi.

"I am ready to die," Arjun declared defiantly.

"Why die? Why not write a letter?"

"Letter?"

"If she replies, you two could run away," Adi suggested.

Recess ended as the girl finished the eleventh tomato. Mrs. Nargis rang the bell and started teaching the history lesson. Under normal circumstances she was a conventional teacher, but that day her lecture took an unconventional turn.

"Class," she began in a subdued voice, "over there on the distant mountains, there are two gardens. On the left is Shalimar and on the right is Nishat. Shalimar was built by the Emperor for the Empress. And Nishat was built by the Empress's brother for the Empress."

"Yes, Madam," boomed the boys. Arjun watched the girl eat her thirteenth tomato.

"One day, in A.D. 1632, the Emperor cut off the supply of water to Nishat. Do you know why?"

"No, Madam!"

"Because Nishat was as beautiful as Shalimar."

"Yes, Madam," chimed the boys. Adi studied the girl as she started on her fourteenth tomato.

Arjun half-listened to the history of gardens. He was busy drafting a love letter with a blue pencil. When the epistle was done, he asked Adi for editorial assistance. Adi used the eraser generously and added a few lines.

"How are you going to hand it to her?" whispered Adi.

"I'll walk to her chair."

"Fool, do it with style."

Adi transformed the declaration of love into a messenger plane and propelled it upward as Mrs. Nargis chalked some new history on the blackboard.

Arjun saw the entire class twist their necks. The boys turned to observe the loops of the plane, which swished out of the tent and returned smelling of saffron. Once inside, the messenger plane, sailing like a bird, sheared past Mrs. Nargis's beehive hair and lost momentum, landing serenely on three tomatoes.

"Girl," said Mrs. Nargis angrily with hands on her hips, "bring it to me."

The girl did exactly as she was told.

The teacher snatched the aircraft from her, flattened its paper, and began reading the blue words to the whole class.

Half-paralyzed, Arjun turned toward Adi. Arjun's eyes shook with alarm.

I love you like in the movies.

Adi sniffled and scuffed his boots against the floor.

I want to marry you. You will be my Empress. I will build you a garden more beautiful than Nishat. We will plant tomatoes in the garden so that you can eat them. Write soon and wait for the next stage of my plan to rescue you.

Flying kiss, Emperor Adi

Arjun heaved a sigh of relief. Adi hid his face between his arms on the desk. Caught by Mrs. Nargis. Caught by his fast friend.

"Girl," asked the teacher rolling her eyes, "do you want to marry Emperor Adi?"

The girl blushed and held her belly and vomited a sweet-smelling paste of tomatoes. Then she wept a flood of tears and ran out of the tent in the direction of the distant moutains. The teacher caned Adi on the back of his hand. She made him wear a chicken mask. She forced him to raise his arms above his head for the rest of the day.

An eerie silence stilled the tent.

Arjun contemplated the situation for a while, his gaze fixed on the two uneaten tomatoes. He knew for certain the girl would return with her father, who would shoot them both: Mrs. Nargis and Adi.

~

Hair

In Kashmir our house stood by a pebbled street. Winter covered the pebbles with snow and all streets looked alike. Distant mountains burned like welding torches.

It was the fortieth winter of the war between India and Pakistan when Mother broke the news: "Adi, your father is dead."

Her hands were trembling for me because I was only nine and I didn't know the meaning of death. Father was swallowed by an avalanche, she said, which was triggered by the bloody Tuesday crossfire. After ten days the rescue party gave up the search. They returned with his khaki turban, two medals, a name-plate, and polished boots. Mother and Lily Aunty cried and cried and filled our house with Father's stories. They decided to preserve his memories by locking his study and the laboratory.

Mother forgot to shut the ventilator, my secret way into the lab. Inside, pungent benzene vapor floated like a kite separated from a string. Spider webs invaded the Erlenmeyer flasks and Bunsen burners and other equipment, all except the bandaged microscope, which I used to examine molecules. Father had bandaged the microscope to guard it against the mountain weather. He was an army chemist in the intelligence wing of the Sikh regiment; everybody called him the Sardar-of-all-trades.

"Kashmir will kill us with *barbaric* cold even if we escape shelling," Lily Aunty complained.

She visited us twice a week; Father's elder sister, an ancient woman with a twisted mouth and a smell of trout.

"For the sake of your boy's future move to the Plains. They are considerably safer, and certainly they don't lack Convent schools."

Mother listened silently. She rarely intervened. She was hardly thirty years old.

"Your boy plays with that betel-nut chewing Ayah of yours," said Lily Aunty. "Not a word of English she knows. Don't blame me if he becomes a Baa-Boo."

Sunday mornings Ayah washed my long hair with Shikakai soap, after which we played cricket. The cork ball hit the ground and bounced snow flakes on us and speckled the bat with slush. Ayah bowled deadly gugglies and I sent the ball flying full-toss.

For wickets we used the solitary apple tree between our house and the next, its identical twin, which had been vacant for a long time and smelled of sour wool; its reddish brown bricks sagged under the weight of corrugated asbestos.

During the break in the War a stranger moved into the house.

The new owner changed the place utterly. At times vapors of sandalwood wafted towards our house. I longed to meet the mysterious person, but she rarely stepped out on the verandah.

"She is a widow," Ayah said.

"Who is a *widow*?"

"Your mother, too, is a widow."

Mother and Lily Aunty called on the neighbor once, but they were not suitably impressed.

"Thinks she is Queen Noor Jahan. Nakhray-walli has long eyelashes."

"Pretends she can speak English like Angrez-log."

The neighbor hired Ayah part-time.

"And now she has snatched our Ayah away."

Late in the evenings Ayah used to walk into the house with that tobacco smell of hers to pack our Bukhari with coal. We could only afford to heat one room in the house. Mother's room. Before it smoldered steadily, the Bukhari sent sulfur-yellow smoke out of the room through a rusty pipe. For us Ayah was several things in one; a cleaning-washing-cooking-Bukhari-milk lady. The neighbor was perhaps trying to save some money because she hired Ayah only as a milk lady. Every evening Ayah walked five miles to the dairy on Old Airport Road to fetch milk for both houses.

I first saw HER the day Ayah fell sick. I was outside drying my long hair. The snow on the street gleamed with confidence. She stepped out on her verandah gathering the loose folds of her pheran. A white shoulder-length scarf covered her head down to her eyebrows. She called me and asked if Ayah was around.

"Mother took her to the hospital," I replied. "It's pneumonia."

"Dékho. One must be careful. Cold winds come from the Nanga Glacier."

"But *nanga* means naked."

"Don't you know? It is in Pir Panjal."

I loved the way she said Pir Panjal. Dimples formed on her cheeks while she spoke slowly in dulcet voice. Her face lit up with the evening light that lingered on the mountains.

"I can't bring the milk on my own," she continued.

"And why can't you?"

"You are too young to understand. The men at the dairy whistle when I go."

"Let me bring milk for you."

"But you don't have your turban on."

"At my age it is allowed."

"Come in then, my dear. You will need the milk can."

I noticed she was barefoot. I followed her to the doorway. The reddish-brown brick walls of her house were wet on the inside; the ceiling leaked at one corner.

"Come in... Chai for you? I have some leftover milk for tea."

"Mother says tea will turn me black."

She laughed until her eyes closed.

"I see you spend long hours in the laboratory. If you would like, why not do an experiment?"

Her living room was lined with little figurines of gods and goddesses, Hindu gods and goddesses. Big portraits of holy men hung on the white-washed walls.

Are Hindus ever going to make up their mind, Mother murmured in my mind, *they have eighty-four million gods and gurus. Our guru is One. And He is our holy book. Remember, never, never, lose faith in Sikhism.*

"How lovely girl-like long hair you've got," she said, handing me tea which smelled of fennel.

"Father had hair more beautiful than mine."

"Ah..."

"My hair can't be more beautiful than yours?"

My remark silenced her; she pursed her lips. During the prolonged silence she kept tapping the empty cup of tea. In the end she said, "I'll pray for Ayah tonight."

The dairy reeked of ammonia. On the way, I discovered a strand of her hair, glued to the milk-can. I unglued the strand and ran it between my thumb and forefinger again and again. Back home I stoppered the specimen in a vial and stored it in Father's lab.

School was off the next day because our teacher was sick. He was a kind and stubbled Muslim man who had taught me the laws of Viscous Fluids. He had also explained to me the physics of snow, hydrogen bonds, why ice floats on water. And it was he who had taught me how to use a microscope.

"No school, but you are staying in," said Mother. Outside large hydrogen-bonded flakes were swirling with mad intensity. "You are going to recite the religious books." I hid Amar-Chitra-Katha comics in between the holy books, but the fact is that I could not even focus on the comics. All day I longed to hear the neighbor's footsteps on the verandah, listen to her say "Pir Panjal." And I was prepared to wait till she answered my secret prayer. I spent hours, my nose glued to the window pane, unable to think or feel coherently.

"You never seemed so interested in blowing snow."

"But Mother…"

"We are off to the hospital."

"Mother, what about the storm?"

"Open your eyes. It stopped long ago."

Mother held my hand and we walked two miles to deliver food for Ayah. Dal, roti, subzi. I carried the hair-vial in my pocket. The Old Airport Road was clogged by noisy vendors praising piles of snowcrusted apples. Ill-fed boys shoved tabloids in our hands. We passed the ammonia-smelling slums by the green lake. On the slushy Zero Bridge an angry crowd doused kerosene on a public bus and set it aflame, shouting "Freedom!" Even Mother didn't know the reason for the crowd's anger.

In the street by the walls of the hospital veiled women wept. Their young sons and daughters were dead, Mother told me. The walls were covered by Binaca toothpaste ads and Quit Kashmir slogans. I picked up a pebble from the street and scribbled on the wall: Pir Panjal.

In the hospital corridor people appeared and disappeared like butterflies. I noticed several women with radium in their eyes disappear through a door reserved for special cases. Ayah was in

Ward No. 6, looking weak and weary.

"Found a new cricket companion?" she asked.

"Don't want to play with anyone else," I replied.

"What is in the glass vial?" she asked as the nurse wrapped her in a red blanket.

"A specimen."

Back home, Mother announced that she had finished reciting the holy book, all 1430 pages, at the rate of 4.054794520548 pages per day. She said she was going to celebrate the event by singing Shabads. She asked Lily Aunty to accompany her on a sitar. She forced me to play the tabla drums.

"I'm off to the dairy," I said abruptly.

"I know why you are interested in the dairy," said Mother. "You bring milk for her. No one needs to bring milk for her."

"At least let me go hike in the mountains."

Lily Aunty raised her hands. She complained that I was beginning to loaf around.

"At your age your father knew science books by heart."

Unable to utter a response I sulked in the corner like a child, while Mother and Lily Aunty gossiped endlessly. Even Mother gossiped with bile in her voice.

"She's dark. Not even wheatish."

"Her features are nice though."

"But she smokes. She will die of smoking."

"I don't like the way she laughs around with the doctors at the regiment hospital."

"She's a magic-garnee."

"She is spoiling our Ayah, makes her sit on the sofa."

"So miserly she is; why doesn't she use Ayah for washing-cleaning-ironing?"

"She killed her husband. Captain Kaul was a gem of a man."

"Wasn't that a plane crash?"

"Captain Kaul and his mother were unhappy with this chudrail witch."

"The plane crashed in Bimbar Gali?"

"No, in Krishna Ghati, was it?"

"In Pir Panjal."

I woke up in the middle of the night mumbling *Pir Mahal di Panjal*. Mother's eyes were sealed with sleep and she was snoring. I lifted my pillow, retrieved the hair-vial, tiptoed out of the heated room towards the lab. I lit up a smoke in the lab. Ayah had taught me how to clench a cigarette and suck the smoke from the top of my fist.

The glow of my Marlboro cigarette illuminated the glass. Inside the vial the strand of hair fluoresced. I transferred it to a glass slide on Father's microscope. Fuzzy honeycombs made up the entire filament. And the molecules—the molecules jostled like lunar dust, rebelling like the masses on the Old Airport Road, murmuring. There were real tears in my eyes; I wiped them with Father's bandage. I yearned for the dark folds of her pheran, and *Freedom*.

I stepped outside. The asbestos roof of her house rattled in the wind. My breath fogged up my glasses; my teeth chattered. The flood of yellow light, emerging from her bedroom window, lit the ice-coated branches of the apple tree. The icicles hanging from the tree looked like the nose of her favorite god, Ganesha. Small icicles formed in my own nostrils. Her window was covered with frozen ferns and ghostly crystals of frost. I crept close to the rusty Bukhari pipe. On the bottom left of the window, heat from the pipe had melted a circle, which looked like the eyepiece of the microscope.

I peeked inside.

She was lying on her bed. Arms folded on chest. Eyes wide open. She was breathing heavily. The saffron quilt dangled from the bed. A pillow was on the carpet. She didn't have her headscarf on. She didn't have any hair.

Who could have hurled such violence on her? Who could have been so cruel to her? Mother and Lily Aunty were certainly cruel to her, but their brand of cruelty was confined to words. On her bed, even without hair, she looked beautiful, like an Amar-Chitra-Katha apsara, while the young moon awoke behind me on the distant mountains. Soon the circle was fogged-up by my breath and I grew dizzy and rushed back.

Her window was heavily shielded with curtains after that night. Because of me snow inched up like a hideous wall between the two twin houses. Because of me the apple tree transformed into an ever-vigilant sentry. And she: Her absence seemed interminable. And me: Guilt stung me wherever I went.

The following day I heard Mother crying in the kitchen. The milk had curdled overnight.

"Mother, I don't like milk anyways."

"Look at your face. How will you grow up?"

"But I don't want to grow up."

"What is bothering you? Why are you hiding things from me?"

The day Ayah returned home, I defied Mother's orders and knocked on the neighbor's door. She appeared on the verandah after a long time. She'd grown weak and weary like Ayah; her lips were parched.

Leaning on the rail she asked, "Have you been smoking?"

I didn't know what to say.

"In your religion boys are not allowed to smoke."

Silence.

"Why are you standing there like a sheep? Come in."

She guided me to her living room where she looked at me for a long time. She took my hand and the next moment threw it aside and turned towards the kitchen. It was then I noticed she'd rearranged the Ganesha figurines since my last visit.

She returned from the kitchen with an incense stick, which she kept rolling through her fingers. Suddenly she held my hand. Once again she looked at me for a long time. "Tomorrow, will you take me to the lake?" she asked. "I would like to sit inside the lake. Only in water is there some peace."

"But," I said, "the lake is cold. Water steals heat from our bodies thirty times faster."

"Will you or won't you?"

"Mother doesn't want me to go near the lake. It is only a mile from the trenches."

"Sometimes," she said, "the war is within us."

"What do you mean?"

"There is a kind of war," she said, "that no microscope can see."

She disentangled our hands.

"Cancer," she said. "You are too young to understand."

"Teach me how to tie a turban," she said. "I would like to visit the lake tomorrow with the turban on."

I had no time to remind her that in my religion turbans were for boys and men only. While I tied the yard of cloth around her head she sat still and looked at me through long eyelashes, and I felt like saying something to her, but couldn't. So I wept. For no reason an image of Father returned to me, and for a second the lake looked like a dead peacock. Cold and green. Dancing. Mixing. Separating. Wounding me wherever I went.

~

Border Cricket

Eleventh of October was a perfect day for cricket. The blush on the chenar leaves, the brilliance of colors, the fragrance of irises, everything encouraged us to leave bed early and unearth our red leather balls and varnished willow bats. Without opening our eyes we knew perfectly well that it was going to be a great day for cricket.

"Wake up, boys," said Mother with milk glasses tinkling on her tray. "Today, you must learn the rules of the game from your uncle."

"Fantastic," we said while sipping milk. So it was finally going to happen. Mother's brother, Sardar Ranjit Singh, a retired cricket umpire, was on his way to Kashmir. Uncle Ranji, we called him in short. He had umpired twelve matches in London, Jamaica, Lahore. Only he knew how to calculate the velocity of cricket balls at 5,000 feet above sea level a thousandth of a second ahead of us.

"Hurry up, boys!"

"What time is Uncle Ranji arriving?"

"He is already here," she said. "Behave this time."

Together, we ran down the steps to meet him.

The man sitting on the sofa had pure gray in his hair. One of his eyes protruded like a precious stone in a sixteenth-century ring. This was the result of a past cricketing accident in Pakistan.

Although the stone eye was as wide as the good eye, it gave his face the look of a Mughal garden in early stages of ruin; not the man whose dashing pictures we used to scan now and then in Mother's black-and-white album. Yet he wore white flannel trousers and a dark blazer and stood up as we approached.

"Who are you?" he asked.

"Champions," we said, giving him a hug and a bouquet of narcissi.

"You boys have grown up fast," he said. "This is the best height for playing cricket."

"Coach us."

"Sorry Baba. Didn't your mummy tell you? This time I am here to be the umpire for the one-day match between India and Pakistan."

We had a bit of trouble following him.

"But, Uncle," we asked, "you are retired, no?"

His youngest daughter, the one with very large ears, had accompanied Uncle Ranji. Sitting on the settee, she grimaced, almost coughed at our question. She was very careful about her fashionable skirt.

"Baba, I was recalled from retirement," explained Uncle Ranji. "The umpire originally chosen by the Board was killed by the terrorists—"

"Don't speak such things in front of boys," interjected Mother.

Uncle simply ignored her like a pebble. "Like your mummy, all umpires were afraid," he said. "No one was willing to replace the dead man. The Chief of Cricket spoke to me personally."

He mimicked...

"Chief goes: 'The match must carry on. Orders from top.'

"I go: 'But there is violence in the valley.'

"Chief goes: 'Cricket will give the valley a human face.'

"I go: 'At my age one is not afraid of dying.'"

We felt very sorry for Uncle Ranji.

"Don't worry, Uncle, we'll be your bodyguards."

"They are only boys," pleaded Mother. "Let's talk about other things."

Mother treated us like baachay-kids, much to our annoyance. Arjun, my friend, was as strong as me. He was an ace bowler and myself, a dashing batsman. We were self-taught cricketers, having acquired the art along steep slopes, on frozen lakes, inside school buses.

The short day quickly turned into dusk and we had yet to begin. After he was well rested, Uncle Ranji donned a felt hat and drove us toward the stadium. Mother was not very pleased with the idea that we accompany him, but he insisted. "Everything is in Guru's hands," he assured her while rubbing his hands briskly. "Plus, I have appointed these army brats of yours as my security guards." He drove the Mahindra & Mahindra jeep. A cold wind was blowing in the valley, speeding toward us from the gap in the mountains, curling our hair.

"Are you afraid of the militants?" we asked from the back seat. "Jokes apart," he replied, "those lumpens are the last things on my mind, but certainly I am afraid of your cousin. I am afraid of what she will do in life."

His youngest daughter had stayed at home with Mother. "She is difficult," he clarified. "She hates cricket. After thirteen, she started hating everything. When she runs out of things to hate, she hates me and her mother. She should have come with us tonight. The air of Kashmir is so fresh and clear. Like a flower."

We were only a mile away from the stadium, next to an abandoned bunker, when Uncle Ranji applied the emergency brakes. The jeep squeaked to a halt.

Suddenly four veiled women pressed revolvers against our ears. Woman No.1 gripped Uncle Ranji's arm and transferred him to the rear seat. He did not resist, but his stone eye flickered.

Woman No. 2 extracted a cricket ball from his blazer. She spat over the red ball and rubbed it against her black veil. The ball acquired the shine of a nocturnal apple. She offered the ball back to him on her palm. Uncle looked down at the ball, but did not touch it.

"You all will put on these glasses," instructed Woman No. 3. Nothing was visible through the dark glasses. Woman No. 4 sat at the wheel and switched on the radio.

"Where are you taking us?" asked Uncle Ranji nervously.

"You will find out," said the kidnappers.

When the jeep stopped, the veiled women led us through a noisy door.

"This is it," they said. "Remove your glasses."

We found ourselves in the courtyard of a gloomy, timber-framed building from the time of the British, roosters flying in the air. The place smelled of mules and sheep. A campfire burned in the middle of the courtyard. Huge pipette shaped flames. Four new women, middle-aged, with a military air, clapped their hands.

We almost fainted with fear, but it was too late, and it was very cold.

The women flaunted their Uzi machine guns. They were vicious types. Not for an instant did they take their eyes off Uncle Ranji. They were like the ogresses in the Mahabharata, who had come after the Pandavas during their exile in the salt mines of Kashmir.

A little girl stepped out of the kitchen with a samovar and served us salt tea. A thin glaze of salt crystals had accumulated under her fingernails.

"Who are you people?" asked Uncle Ranji, angrily.

"We will tell," said the leader, stretching her hands to the fire. "First drink tea."

The girl filled eight cups.

"Salaam," the leader spoke from behind the smoke. "They call me Zoon."

"What is the meaning of this?" asked Uncle. "Tell us, Zoon." The last bit he said as if he knew her well.

"Finish your tea first," she said.

The little girl blinked her eyes. She was listening curiously, her fingers half dipped in the bowl of salt. Zoon pulled out a twig from the fire and poked it inside the bowl, which stirred the girl's fingers. The twig was no longer a piece of wood. It was studded with crystals, all glittering like diamonds.

"Our men are foolish," said Zoon. "Tomorrow they plan to wave Pakistani flags at the stadium. So we women have decided to act."

"You kidnapped us," said Uncle.

"We did not kidnap you. You all are free to go," said Zoon. "We did kidnap your youngest daughter."

"O God, Wahé-Guru! Where is she?"

"Girl is not here. But, you can save her. You must help India win tomorrow's cricket match. Bring Pakistan to its knees."

"Why?" asked Uncle Ranji, screening his face from fire with the sleeve of his blazer.

"Because the army commandos will burn our streets and houses if India loses."

Saying this Zoon tapped the twig on the ground. The crystals fell. The twig was twig again.

"If you betray us," she warned, " your daughter—"

Uncle Ranji, the man famed for his integrity, bit the skin around his nails until they bled. Zoon and her companions made us wear the dark glasses and drove us close to the stadium. "Remember," they said. Uncle didn't speak a word. He put his hand out. They did not shake it.

The Bulbul stadium stood on a hill like a citadel. Bulbul—so called because the red granite and glass structure with 'wings' was built on the site of a demolished birdhouse that once belonged to the Maharajah. Inside the stadium, the area between the oval and the stands was packed with multicolored ads twittering to each other. *Now even in a nappy a baby is happy. Amul butter salutes our soldiers at the border. Dip, dip, dip, and you are ready to sip: Taj Mahal Tea.*

The stadium was shrouded that night by a whole battalion of army commandos. Uncle Ranji had to produce two i.d.s to get in. We stumbled along. The brass buttons on his blazer glistened in the floodlights as he performed the Cricket Board specified tests.

"Dead," he said, tapping his willow bat on the pitch. "This ground is worthless. Feel it, feel it with your hands, Baba. Too much spongy it is. Tomorrow this two-rupee sponge will dictate the outcome of the game. Not fair for the player. Not fair for my daughter."

Back home, Uncle drank rum.

"Two women came to use the phone," said Mother. "They—"

"I don't want to listen to any of that," said Uncle. "I refuse to be blackmailed by a bunch of pagal-mad women."

There was indescribable intensity in his eyes.

Mother prayed to gods from four religions. We, too, tried hard to stop the night.

At eight in the morning a line of windowless armored cars came scudding into the stadium. The cars stopped close to the ancient chenar trees. Twenty-two players sprang out and raced to the metal detectors. We witnessed the spectacle along with Umpire Ranji from inside the stadium gates. Something in the stride of those overgrown boys reeked of rupees. They were not Indians or Pakistanis; they were from the country of rupees—eleven from this side of the border, and eleven from over there. We felt like kidnapping one of them. But our breath was coming out hard, with a wheeze.

Handsome army commandos with sub-machine guns marched in after the players. A whole battalion filled the space between the ads and the chalked boundary. Red, disfigured leaves swirled around the flag posts, and the wind howled like a pack of dogs. Small leaves drifted out of the oval, in the direction of the invisible mountains, and the place looked needlessly beautiful.

At 9 AM, sharp, the Beauty Queen inaugurated the match. She performed a poem by Habba Khatoon and said, "This match is for peace." The crowd cheered. She said, "Cricket is a serene sport and cricket spectators are the most well behaved in the world." The crowd whistled. She said, "Now all of you stand up for the two national anthems." No one stood up.

Mohammed-A, the Indian captain, won the toss and elected to bowl first. The Pakistani batsmen made a stellar start. Three sixes during three consecutive balls. Now and again men in pherans raised green Pakistani flags, emitting chants of political protest, mostly sympathizing with the enemy team. Veiled women raised the Indian tri-color; some, the Kashmiri flag. Raucous songs filled the entire stadium.

During the twentieth over, the Indian players appealed "Howzat!! Out!! L.B.W."

Now was the perfect time for Umpire Ranji to save his youngest daughter. He stood still for a long time before delivering the verdict.

"NOT OUT!" he announced finally with high integrity.

The Indian team screamed "cheeeeeaaaaat" at the decision.

We, too, felt like screaming at Uncle Ranji. Had he lost his mind? Aunty Ranji and the two older daughters and the son in Southall, London, were never going to spare him if he ended up killing his daughter.

But the thirtieth over brought a sharp turn; things began to heat up. Five of the best Pakistani batsmen were sent to the pavilion for a single run by the medium pacers, bowling at the speed of 86.3 miles per hour. The crowd stopped cheering. Only a sigh here, a shriek there.

We stood on our seats in the East wing of the stadium. Right above us, in a glass cubicle, a man from Radio Kashmir was delivering the ball-by-ball commentary. Our Japanese transistor set hummed with his stealthy voice, injecting waves of mystery into our ears.

Clean-bowled! Clean-bowled! The Pakistani innings collapsed with this ball. The Paki's put on a whopping 171 for the loss of seven wickets after fifty overs. All eyes, now, set on India. Situation is critical but not serious.

During the lunch break, Uncle Ranji was invited by the radio commentator to his booth for an interview. The Beauty Queen, with pencil eyebrows, was the commentator's second guest. Uncle was seated for a while next to her shaved legs.

Commentator: The Pakistanis have finished solidly despite the fiasco.

Beauty Queen: Tell us, Mr. Ranji, your honest opinion about the match so far.

Umpire Ranji: It is a most disappointing match because the pitch is dictating the outcome of the game. One could argue with the benefit of hindsight that it was a bad decision on India's part to allow Pakistan to bat first.

Beauty Queen: Yes or no, can India win the match?

Umpire Ranji: The pitch will work against them.

Beauty Queen: All competitions, Mr. Ranji, need winners and losers. Ha!

Umpire Ranji: I know, but this one is not good for my health.

Commentator: We shall all drink to your health after the match is over. Thank you for being with us.

Uncle Ranji headed for the pavilion like a slain Maharajah. That is when we lost contact with him. He told us, days before he died, that inside the dressing-room a tiny packet, wrapped in parchment, was waiting for him. He opened the packet with extreme agility and caution, but the substance inside the packet fell at his feet, revealing a whorl of flesh. The edges were heavy with a layer of dry, congealed blood. He picked up the whorl and read the note stapled to the inner edge. "Father, this is my left ear. Zoon thinks you have forgotten your promise. Please don't betray us."

The old man closed his solitary eye and thought of Lord Shiva. Long ago, Lord Shiva had inadvertently beheaded his own son. And long ago, Lord Shiva had managed to attach an elephant's head to his son. "At that moment, Baba, I felt more anger than pain. I felt like kidnapping all twenty-two players, announcing the event on the radio, forcing the match to a close. Anything to save a life. But the reputation of Indian umpiring was at stake. I chose cricket. Integrity I chose."

Match resumed. India lost both opening batsmen within the first four overs. The lightening demise of the third player made the Indian team appeal the umpire's verdict.

But Ranji's upraised finger did not bend.

India threatened to abort the match.

The crowd whistled, booed, howled and sent down hostile slogans.

We waited for divine intervention. Hours passed. The Indians recovered. Batting at number six and seven, Mohammed-A and the pugnacious all-rounder Harjot-S rescued the underdogs. The flashing blade of their bat gave the Indian scorecard the respectability it deserved.

35

The match was headed for a tight finish.

With only seven balls to go, India needed four runs to triumph. It was then Harjot-S was caught and bowled by a Pakistani leg spinner. The crowd cheered and waved huge enemy flags. We almost burst into tears. And we couldn't see a thing. Tall men and veiled women in the rows ahead of us stood up. We raised the transistor set to our ears. The commentator's voice was becoming faster, more alert, exact.

Shadows are lengthening on the field. The final moments of this epic are approaching. Last ball. Delivered by a left-arm spinner. And the Indian captain Mohammed-A, the hope of the nation, has hit it to the boundary. HOWZAT! HOWZAT! Ball headed for a four. India will never forgive, sorry, forget this four. That is if it is a four. NOOOO! Oh Noooo! SHIT. Pardon my language, ladies and gentlemen— A terrible mishap— A terrible mishap— Umpire Ranji, yes, the umpire is lying on the ground. Flat on the ground. The ball hit him on the way to the boundary. Orange shirts. Orange shirts are bulleting through the oval with a stretcher. They've put Ranji on the stretcher. He fell like an autumn leaf... If he is dead this match will have to end in a draw. When we spoke to Ranji during lunch, he looked frail. Umpire Ranji started his career in South Africa and just prior to his retirement, during the World Cup series in Lahore, Pakistan, he lost an eye. Here was a man.... The stretcher has made it to the gates. I am watching the stretcher with the zoom of my cameraman. There is a hush in the crowd... The umpire—. Yes, the umpire just stirred on the stretcher. He, he, he just lifted his hand up in the air. He waved. He waved! Five thousand veiled women are waving back, ears glued to their transistor sets. Yes, folks, my cameraman just confirmed... It is a f-o-u-r! The umpire just signalled a four from the stretcher. He waved his arm from side to side. Yes! Men in pherans are hurling ripe fruits toward the stretcher. India has won an excellent victory! Pakistan is beaten, but not disgraced.

Ladies and gentlemen, although dusk has descended on the Bulbul stadium, I am glad to report that CRICKET is alive and kicking. On this historic evening, cricket is the real winner.

We darted through the crowd to the army ambulance. But the paramedics insisted they did not want baachay-kids in the vehicle. "She is alive, she is alive," the umpire muttered during that brief encounter. "Baba, make sure she forgives me."

Red and yellow leaves rolled behind the ambulance. Outside the stadium, the jumpy commandos marched to the food stalls to celebrate. Vendors were stirring salt in freshly brewed tea. *Two for one! Two for the price of one!* Close by on a bench, a one-eared girl was painting in the shadows of the passing crowd. And it seemed as though in a little while a new match would begin.

"Hurrah!" we said.

~

Nooria

A little girl was sitting on a rock at the edge of a lake, her feet entangled with weeds and lilies. She was eating tomatoes and looking at herself eating. The lake was intensely green, almost still. Now and then the stillness made urgent attempts to speak to her.

"Nooria! Nooria!"

Her mother's heavy voice came from inside the houseboat.

Nooria finished her last tomato and captured a frog hopping on the rock. The frog quivered, then froze, while trying to speak to her. She ran her finger on the blue circles that rimmed the creature's wide-open eyes. Its skin was black and rusty, just like the metal over the houseboat.

"Nooria! Nooria! Your father wants to see you right away."

The girl drew her feet back from the water and placed the frog on the glaringly white rock. She ran as fast as she could, one hand glued to thick glasses, the other clutching the schoolbag, past a hazy figure in the smoke-filled kitchen—mother peeling roots of lotus. Her Abba's room was the largest in the boat, the one that did not leak.

Ever since losing his leg, Abba remained inside. An encounter with the army had anchored him forever. Always he sat upright on his bed. Always he kept a little pot with charcoal embers, the kangri, under his cloak. Nooria didn't believe all the things the boys at school said about him. Abba was nice.

"You returned early from school?" he asked from his bed.

"Teacher declared full break."

"Tell me the truth, girl," he demanded. "If you lie again I will throw this kangri at your face."

She dumped the bag on the floor.

"Girl, look at me, not at the TV."

"Abba, teacher said after recess there won't be classes. A guest speaker will lecture on something not in our syllabus."

"You will put on your shoes and you will pick up your bag and you will go to the school right now," he said. "Listen to the man and then return and tell me all. Fast. If you lie again, girl, something terrible will happen. Terrible."

"Abba—"

Her father's attention drifted to the news scrolling on the television screen.

"Nooria! Nooria! It is cold. Don't forget your pheran."

She ran back to the school, which was on the other side of the lake. From the schoolyard the long chains of mountains looked blissful most of the year, but in winter they resembled skulls of snow. Between the yard and the mountains there were elderly apple trees—big reddish-green fruits hanging in the air. Strange school it was with a childish name—Little Flower Central School. She wished to lose it—lose it the way she lost her gloves last winter.

Little Arjun was her only ally in the class. So different he was from the galaxy of other boys—all bullies.

They had asked, "Nooria, is your belly black?"

"No," she had said.

"Show us."

"No."

"Her belly is black, her belly is black, she won't show us!"

"Leave her alone," Arjun had said. But the brigadier's son hit her on the nose.

Some people are violent and make others violent—her Abba had told her. Never bend to look at the color of your belly—her Ammi had told her. Nooria never examined her belly. Not even inside the houseboat. Nooria and her Ammi and Abba lived in the boat because the waves of tourists had stopped visiting Kashmir. Ammi sold all the princely furniture in the boat. The only precious thing remaining was a black-and-white Sony television, the one Uncle installed after her father lost his leg. Abba always complained and always watched the television, which seemed to have replaced his missing leg. He once forced Ammi to cook something other than lotus roots. Ammi said that the only things left to cook were the rocks. Ammi never complained. She slept on the smelly carpet on the floor; only Abba had a bed. To keep warm they burned chenar leaves in little earthenware hearths. On cold nights Nooria, like her parents, placed the hearth on her belly. The kangri had charred her belly into painful arabesques. Of course, her belly was black.

Late for the lecture, she stood at the entrance of a shamiana tent, pitched around the temporary playground. Behind her the brick-and-cement classrooms were empty. She had never seen the entire school packed so tightly in a tent, elbows touching.

Teacher was on the stage. "Children," she said, "the guest lecturer is our country's most famous scientist, the father of bombs and missiles."

Nooria thought, "The Missile Man doesn't look scary at all."

He resembled a cartoon character in the comic books. Buck teeth. Long, grizzled hair. Shirt untucked. Rubber sandals. Now, standing behind the microphone with a huge parrot on his shoulder.

"Children," said the Missile Man in a booming voice, "Once upon a time Kashmir was a beautiful lake. A lake as large as the sea. And once upon a time there lived a monster by the lake. He poisoned the lotus flowers floating on the lake. People were so miserable, they prayed and prayed to the heavens. Finally, Goddess Parvati opened her eyes and drained the lake by dropping mountains on the monster."

The teacher, sitting on a tin chair behind the speaker, laughed like a doll. Her deep blue sari laughed along.

"How many of you children believe this story?" asked the Missile Man.

All boys raised their hands. Nooria kept her hands in her pockets.

"That is why," explained the Missile Man, "our country is not developed. We don't believe in physics, we believe in stories, which are lies. We should believe in tek-no-logy. Technology will wake up our souls. Missiles will make our country great. Missiles will give us dignity."

An electromagnetic pulse went through the pupils. The Missile Man's words were spreading radially from his mouth and inundating the tent. Propelled by alcohol and liquid oxygen, his words were hitting their eardrums: "Children, we are a country of a billion people, we must develop missiles for a billion people." He was transforming into tin as he was speaking, his teeth glazing like aluminum, and from a distance he looked like a flaming arrow on a launch pad.

Nooria took off her shoes. She turned them and shook the pebbles out on the carpet and rubbed her cold feet. The lake had left an itch on her toes, strange marks on them.

"Children, the day we launch our own Made-in-India missile,

we will irreversibly join the club of advanced nations. That day people all over the world will bow in front of us and envy the sweet fruits of our development. It can happen any day now, I am very optimistic—then you will be able to look the American children in the eye. You will walk with chin high."

Applause!

The teacher glided from her metal chair to the microphone. "Children, Doctor-Professor S. is not only an accomplished scientist, he is a multifaceted man, a complete man. When he is not designing weapons he is cooking vegetables or playing the most enchanting ragas. We are so fortunate today because Doctor-Professor S. has brought along with him his instrument, the shehnai, all the way from the capital city.

Applause!

The Missile Man drank a glass of water and unpacked the instrument out of a red velvet case. "Children, now I will perform the *Song of India.*"

Nooria closed her eyes and mouthed the words of the song. Even the birds stopped singing while the man played the shehnai. Only the parrot on the man's shoulder sang along. After a while, the man arose and started moving with agility, his fingers crawling over his instrument. A long line of pupils formed behind him, marching to the weeping willows by the lake.

The pupils formed a spiral behind the Missile Man. Stray dogs and mountain goats joined in. The melody of shehnai kept swelling and shrinking, shrinking and swelling, softly and serenely dropping its notes, filling the valley with ragas and raginis—*Basant, Malahar, Bhairav.* The children, now and then, rearranged themselves into well-disciplined alphabetical formations. A-B-C-D.

D for Dream.

D for Donkey.

D for Development.

Nooria lifted a little dog in her arms and through half-closed eyes and thick glasses saw how the country was already changing into a developed country. She saw thousands of shiny missiles, a whole constellation. And she saw her country opening like a boundless flower. The mountains were becoming rounder, more beautiful, and the cities and towns and villages were rearranging themselves around the streets lit by lamps brighter than light. So much development, and so fast that it was spilling from the lake into people's lips, which were like petals, pulsating with joy. Houseboats were transforming into mansions, and minarets of the mosques into music, and no one was poor and no one was eating rocks any more.

She wept when the Missile Man packed away his instrument and stepped inside a big helicopter. She wept when the Missile Man waved. She waved back. The parrot didn't wave. She wept when the blades on the helicopter blew dust in her eyes.

"Children," said the bird-eyed teacher, "in ancient times our country was very developed. You just have to watch TV to find this out."

"Yes, Madam!" yelled the pupils, scuffing muddy boots against the ground.

The teacher distributed a sheet to each one of the forty-seven pupils.

"This evening you all will watch the ancient epic Mahabharata on TV and all of you will answer the question in the home assignment."

The helicopter blocked the sun above the pupils and suddenly the whole school was covered by an immense shadow.

"And you, Nooria," said the teacher pointing the cane at her, "do you have a TV at home?"

"Yes, Madam."

"Good."

"But Madam," she confessed, "my father doesn't allow me to

watch the shows."

The boys in the back laughed.

"Because you are only a Muslim?" asked the teacher. Her face became a boiling root of lotus, fuelled by the sun, the helicopter no longer visible.

"I will expel you if you come to school without homework tomorrow."

Nooria felt pain in her belly. She couldn't understand the connection between being a Muslim and not watching TV.

Ever since the opthalmologist-without-degree had prescribed her glasses, thick round bottom flask types, her father had cut her TV watching. He didn't know the biology of myopia. "If you ruin your eyes, we will never find a boy to marry you," Abba had said. Ammi didn't say a thing, but she believed Abba. She said Nooria's sins had ruined her eyes. Abba made her feel that watching TV was worse than the combined effect of staring at the sun, a dead man's face, and kissing in films. He invented a strange ritual. She was allowed to face the TV set for a minute after every ten minutes of not-watching. During those ten minutes of not-watching, she was forced to rest her eyes by gazing at the lake.

But how was she going to do the Mahabharata homework this way? She felt like crumpling the teacher's assignment sheet.

"I will help you," little Arjun whispered in her ear.

He told her the plan.

"Let me do your homework," he said.

"No," she said. "I do not want you to do my work."

"In that case, Nooria, you can watch TV at my place."

Her Abba had told her to stay away from the road that led to the military camp. The boy lived in a yellow house on the slopes of Sulphur Mountain. He was a Sikh boy, but really he was a girl. He kept his hair in a knot over his head. Once he had opened the knot and his hair had tumbled down to the ground.

The Missile Man's face followed the girl to her friend's house. From the roof of the house arose a TV antenna, a finger pointing at the sky. The place smelled strange—an orchard of almonds, pine-woods, boot polish. Nooria pinched her nostrils; then took a deep breath. The boy's parents were not home.

"You could have waited to ask your father-mother," said the orderly from the veranda.

"She will leave before they return," the boy assured the orderly.

"Can she watch TV?"

"Maybe."

The long-legged orderly looked at Nooria strangely, his eyes wider than the Missile Man's parrot.

Nooria dumped the bag on the steps. She unhooked her shoes and stood barefoot on the veranda. In the valley below the river gushed and gleamed with confidence. The lake looked like a huge prehistoric fish. "All things look pretty from far away," Ammi had said. On the left of the lake stood her school. Faraway on the frozen mountains she saw hundreds of military trucks, roaring to the camp. Not far from the camp, on the right side of the lake, was an arc of white rocks. Floating by the rocks—a few nervous house-boats. She squeezed her eyes and saw the big TO LET signs on the houseboats, half submerged in water. She heard the lake say something urgently to her. A tremor passed through her spine.

"I must call home."

"It is the same thing," said the boy. "Your father will get angry both ways."

"I want to go home."

"You will have to lie," said the boy.

She called the neighbors. She informed them to tell her Abba that school got extended by an hour.

"Why are you crying, Nooria?" asked the boy after she hung up.

"Something terrible will happen now," she said, "because I

lied. Abba told me something terrible would happen if I lied."

Arjun turned on the television. Nooria's watch showed six o'clock. The Mahabharata serial was still seven minutes away. Nooria dug out the assignment sheet from her pheran pocket.

"Raise the volume."

"Louder!"

"Enough."

Chocolate commercials filled the big colored screen. 'I'm good! I'm tempting! I'm too good to share! What am I? Cadbury's or Kashmir?'

A sharp looking lady delivered the news in English, just like foreign people. "Today at 13:50 hours," she said, "two Made-in-India missiles, Agni and Dhanush, were tested positively."

They clapped. The orderly clapped. They danced. The orderly danced. They skipped on the sofa, transformed it into a noisy trampoline, their heads crowned with Arjun's father's turbans. The sparse-haired orderly had no turban on his head. Nooria did not like the way his eyes whooshed while looking at her. "I like the zigzag pattern on your dress," he pointed out.

"6:07 already! Nooria! Nooria! The assignment!"

She sat on the sofa between the orderly and the boy, watching TV expertly, like her Abba. She giggled at the man in the serial; he resembled the Missile Man. She loved his shiny dress, radiant armor. Why was he so serious? She removed her glasses, wiped them with a hanky.

The Man was playing a game of dice. He was playing and winning-winning the Mahabharata. He won horses and elephants. He won five brothers and their wife, Draupadi. Then he started playing with Draupadi, with her hair, her red sari. He spun her like a top. She turned and turned, so did her sari. Strange sari it was. It kept falling-falling on the floor, kept flooding the palace.

Nooria wanted to see if Draupadi's belly was black. But the sari was limitless. Nooria almost yawned.

Teacher's assignment: What was the length of Draupadi's sari?

[a] −1 m

[b] √ 2 m

[c] 100 m

[d] ∞

[e] 0

Arjun chose [c]. Nooria chose [d].

"Is the Mahabharata true?" asked Nooria. "Abba says it isn't."

"Yes," said the boy with conviction, "it is true."

"How do you know?" she asked, looking at him through her fingers.

"Because it is true, stupid."

The orderly ordered them to stop fighting. "I wish I could help," he said, "but I am no good at maths or history." He unbuttoned his shirt. He exposed his hard teeth, full of gaps. He started rapping his knuckles on the side table. When the boy disappeared to the bathroom the orderly asked Nooria to listen to the sound of the boy's urine hitting the toilet lid. She laughed. The orderly laughed. He removed his shirt and scratched his pants.

"I have a missile too," he said. "Do you want to play with it?"

"No," she said.

Nooria skipped to the veranda. It was getting chilly. Black ribbons were sitting on the lake, ink-colored clouds. She put her hands in the pockets of her pheran. She was confused. She thought missiles were not meant for playing.

Her Abba had told her that something terrible would happen if she lied. She picked up her bag and pressed the glasses on her nose and ran down the hill. She ran without her shoes.

She squeezed past the convoy of huge military trucks. She

splashed cold water on her woollens, wading through the stream. She was afraid of the orderly. She crossed the river jumping seventeen times, from rock to rock. She paid little attention to the ropes of water, striking the rocks. Breaking. The distance to the houseboat felt limitless. She ran past military uniforms drying on the rocks. She ran along the furious lake and paid no attention to the insects screaming on water. Her feet hurt terribly. A pack of dogs growled after her. Faster.

As she was running, her nose streamlined in the wind She felt that all the development her country had attained earlier in the morning was slipping through her fingers. The beautiful belly of development had tilted like the moon, a bit too quickly, before she could rub her cheeks against its charred flesh. She was no longer able to hear the melody of metals, no longer touch the riveted surfaces hidden behind the mountains. And it was all her fault.

She kept running.

"Nooria! Nooria! Where have you been? Why is your pheran wet? Wash your hands. Join your father for dinner."

Abba was sitting upright on his bed, shivering, watching the missiles on the TV.

Ladies and gentlemen, we have with us tonight the saint of science, the father of missiles, true genius, Doctor-Professor S. He will enlighten us about the differences between the ancient Brahmastra in the Mahabharata and the modern Agni weapons.

Applause!

"*Friends, my team has finally developed the fire to ignite the modern Brahmastra. Today we have earned the right to sing the Song of India. But let us not forget that the ancient weapons were simplistic. Our dream is to develop a type-9 device that can fly to an enemy country, deliver the fire and return for another run.*"

Applause!

"A quantum leap, ladies and gentlemen…."

"Why are you crying, Nooria?" asked Ammi.

"I do not like the dogs."

"Stop talking," shouted Abba, "or I will throw the kangri on you."

"Something terrible—" she said, covered with sweat and shivers.

The kangri twitched in her father's hands. The TV crackled.

"Something terrible is going to happen, Abba," she said. "Because I lied."

~

Captain Faiz

He landed in Kashmir as a prisoner of war. He was the first of the new arrivals to be taken to the interrogation center. He stumbled forward, ahead of the guards; his eyes, as they adapted to the world of light, streaming.

Captain Faiz was captured after he and his men from the 5th Light Infantry of the Pakistani Army were abandoned by the top-brass in the frigid peaks of K____, 18,000 feet high. Pakistan had started the war, but India was winning it.

Even in defeat, he appeared to be magnetically handsome. Captivity had had little effect on the glow of his skin and the manic wit in his eyes. His coordination had been impaired, and he had become prone to prolonged spells of silence, but his awareness felt heightened.

On the way to the prison camp, from the rear-end of the military truck, he had realized that he was seeing women, again, for the first time in eleven months and nine days. The women were planting paddy in the terraced fields on the slopes of the Pir Panjal mountains. "They are assessing us," he'd mentioned, "as if we've just returned from the bushes." Other captives around him had laughed. "Laugh now. Go ahead," he'd encouraged them. "Soon the Indians will fry us in hell-fire."

At the base camp, 126 men were handed over to the guards,

who had snapped on their bayonets. After a strip search by Special Forces, the uniforms and boots belonging to the captives were hurled into the lake and they were hosed with icy water and marched to the cells, where the barber shaved them and covered their nakedness with starched kurta-pyjamas, stencilled with POW signs. The air in the cells was mildly stagnant, but carried no trace of the men who had died there.

Special Forces found many items in Captain Faiz's uniform and that is why he was first on the list for questioning.

Colonel Arora, the interrogator, eyes as sharp as a terrier, watched his troops march toward his office with the POW. The troops clicked their heels and saluted him and displayed the captive's possessions on the table. An identity card. A leather wallet. Several secret passwords scribbled in Urdu. A book. The colonel cleared his throat and picked up the book. He probed the table of contents.

"Take everything else away," he pointed at the table. "Label them. Deposit them in a safe. Not a single thing is to be thrown in the lake. Understand?"

"Yes-sir."

The colonel flipped through Captain Faiz's book several times before slipping it in his own pocket. "The captain is staring at us," he said, clearing his throat. "Bring him closer." The prisoner was seized by the elbow and marched to a spot next to the colonel's table.

Colonel Arora stood up. He was astonished. Captain Faiz was the first one for a long time to fearlessly return his gaze. The colonel pulled the captive's book out of his pocket and looked right through big brown eyes.

"Shahid's verse!" he asked. "A poet in the hands of a soldier? In the trenches?"

Captain Faiz didn't utter a word. Only a sigh of relief.

The colonel opened the book again, keeping his head tilted at an angle. He wore a majestic green turban with a red regimental ribbon on it. His beard had many strands of grey.

"Officer, answer me!"

"Sir," said the captain with hesitation, "the collection is called *The Country Without a Post Office*."

"You don't have to tell me. I know Shahid better than anyone else—"

I will die, in autumn, in Kashmir,
and the shadowed routine of each vein
will almost be news, the blood censored,
for the *Saffron Sun* and the *Times of Rain...*

"Pardon me, sir," said the captain, "but I already know that."

"What do you know?"

"Your love for poetry."

"Who are you?" asked the colonel, struck by the unusual response.

"I worked for the ISI," said the captain. "Pakistani Intelligence."

"What else do you know?"

"Everything."

When the guards marched him back to the cell, Captain Faiz tried separating the enlightened colonel 'as he really was' from his profile in the Intelligence files. His initial hunch was correct. He had everything in common with the colonel other than the uniform. This didn't eliminate a set-up. Would he be framed? Or manipulated in some way? The colonel had let him go without much questioning. Was the man acting on his own or obeying orders from the top? He was not surprised when the guard delivered the dal-and-chappati meal in spotless china. Fear, suspicion, agitated his bowels. He prepared himself for everything from torture to a battle of wits. But which would it be this time?

The cell was clean, recently disinfected, lit by an uncovered bulb. He surveyed the white-washed walls. On his left was a map of India, which looked doubly surreal in the attenuated light. While stirring sugar into the tea, he stood facing the map. He was bewitched by the fantastic leaps of imagination made by the cartographer. The whole of Kashmir had shifted into India. He felt like sliding the little mountains and green lakes and pine forests back to Pakistan. He couldn't. The last eleven months had taught him an alternative geography. Kashmir was neither Pakistan, nor India. Kashmir was War.

"Could I get paper and pencil?" he asked the invisible figure posted outside the cell.

The guard brought him a ream of paper, a pencil and another pot of tea. "Colonel-sahib has ordered us to feed you trout from tomorrow onwards."

"Trout?"

This would be it then. A battle of wits.

That night he pinned his faith on poetry. Poetry had saved him from being tortured, the way captives in the adjacent cells were being tortured. Poetry had at least delayed his physical interrogation. That night he wrote his own verses, instead of copying Shahid, which had become a common pastime. The first five poems arrived unexpectedly, like rain. They fell down on paper like stones of hail. He was terrified.

The next day brightened with panic. The mountains awoke quickly, and the lake looked furious.

Colonel Arora met the General Officer Commanding, the GOC, and reported the proceedings at the POW camp.

"We are impressed by your soft methods," said the GOC, adjusting his crowded epaulet. "But more must be accomplished."

"As I reported, sir," said the colonel, "physical interrogation has its limitations."

"Yes, yes," coughed the GOC. "That is what I meant. Invite the bloody bastard to your house, as we discussed. Use scotch and poetry. Make him commit blunders. Reveal the hidden hand of the Pakistani Intelligence."

"But, sir, to my house!" protested the colonel, "I say again. Bringing the prisoner to my home is a ridiculous request. My wife—"

"That is an order," said the GOC.

"Sir, what if the prisoner escapes?" asked the colonel.

"Let him give us his word of honour as an officer that he will not take advantage," said the GOC. "Of course, our boys will be watching too."

Shahid, of whom the GOC had scarcely read a word, was the greatest Kashmiri poet alive. He lived in exile in Amherst, Massachussets, in America. The colonel had stumbled across the poet while decoding a subversive newspaper, the one his soldiers recovered during a raid. He disagreed with the fire-brand politics of the paper, but could not resist the ghazal-like spell of the man's verses. They were not words, they were more like songs for dark times. Only Shahid could evoke the melancholy and the state of unrest in the hills with "a poet's precision and a scientist's passion." And so that day, Colonel Arora was doubly excited about hosting the young Pakistani, who not only knew many things about poetry, but also 'everything' about him. Excited and afraid.

The colonel and his wife resided in the yellow stucco house, on the slopes of Sulphur Mountain. The house was an imitation of the general's mansion, which was larger, more formidable, and stood on a higher level. From the colonel's veranda one could see the valley below, shimmering with lights from the barracks. Approximately two thousand soldiers lived in the barracks, which reeked of rum. The camp was fenced on three sides by barbed wire; on the fourth side was the brimming lake. At the edge of the lake stood a red-tile building, which had lost a wall during the last Pakistani shelling. The bulk of the building remained intact, and had been refurbished as POW cells. A firing range had been laid out adjacent to the cells. Simrita Arora, the colonel's wife, believed that flashes of artillery practice looked like giant incandescent flowers.

"You can *not* bring the enemy home," she said to the colonel.

"But, darling," he said, "Captain Faiz is a poet."

"I don't care," she said. "An enemy is an enemy."

"But darling…," said the colonel.

"Don't say that *darling*," she said, fluffing out the henna-colored hair at her temples. "These days you never say darling. It's been ages since you said *darling. I love you, darling. You are beautiful, darling.*"

"As one grows older," said the colonel, "one says things indirectly—in poetry. One should not *paint* the moon, one should *paint* the shards of glass in which the moon is reflected."

The colonel felt his heart sink while he pedantically explained poetry to his wife. His heart was weak. The condition had not only snatched away his chances for future promotions, but had also robbed him of an active sex life. The doctor had ordered the colonel to sleep in a separate room.

"The doctor has no business in our private life," Simrita Arora had protested initially. But, gradually she accepted the idea and took great pains to furnish her husband's separate bedroom. She ordered embroidered carpets and bedspreads all the way from Srinagar, the capital city. The colonel knew that *excess* was her familiar way to get back at him. Excess and deprivation. Around that time she also became less and less tolerant of his 'bad manners.' No more suppers, no more invitations to fellow officers for garden parties. No more tea and rummy gatherings on the veranda.

The colonel embraced her rules wholeheartedly. He did not share with her the underlying cause of his recent estrangement from the officers in the regiment. A view had formed, largely through rumors, that the colonel's love for poetry had gone too far: "He bribed the doctor to write a fake cardiology report so as to devote himself fully to poetry." The colonel was stunned by the enthusiastic jealousy of his colleagues, Brigadier Atal and Lt. Colonel Thapa. And yet, the GOC seemed to be on his side. The colonel knew too many confidential and *top secret* things. Was that the motive behind the commandant's loyalty? The GOC made sure that the colonel always received soft assignments, like the interrogation of POWs.

"No, you can *not* bring the Enemy home," repeated Simrita Arora. "No."

In some other season Simrita Arora might have led a more independent life. In reality, she didn't have many choices. "There are only three ways for women to sacrifice their lives after marriage," thought Colonel Arora. "Continue working and also work at home. Stop working and only work at home. Or marry a senior army officer."

He had met her during a flight from Kashmir to Delhi. The feminine haughtiness of the air hostess appealed to his heart, and so he composed a poem instead of admiring the Himalayan perspectives through the window. She liked his words. Like him, she had been raised in a decent Sikh family, with a strong presence in the Indian Army right from the time of the British; her grandfather, AVSM, PVSM, double Victoria Cross holder, having trained at the Royal Military Academy, Sandhurst. Technically, their union was labeled an arranged marriage.

Problems began. The new arrival at the army camp didn't get along with other officers' wives. She regarded them as too timid or too overbearing, always complaining about mothers-in-law. So, the colonel manufactured a new life for her; he introduced her to horse-riding and polo.

When she was not riding, she would sit for hours on the veranda reading two-day-old newspapers or in simple contemplation, her gaze fixed on the ancient site in the valley below. She admired the Iron-Age chalk figures etched into the hills behind the mud-and-straw houses. The village, largely inhabited by women, filled the valley with songs and music of the Sufis. Simrita would hear the saddest notes when an occasional man disappeared in compliance with the army's 'catch and kill' campaigns. The widows and other village women were not permitted in the army camp, not even to watch the black-and-white Bombay films, which were screened in the open-air theatre on Saturday nights.

Most army-wallahs considered Smirita Arora a troublemaker. Ten years of marriage and a son, Arjun, hadn't softened that perception. She refused to watch films at the open-air theatre. "I can't imagine sitting along side bidi-smoking soldiers." She chided the GOC at a party for holding a debate on whether the army should shoot women and children suspected of aiding the enemy. When the militants started pouring acid on women's faces for not wearing veils, she asked the army to protect the victims and punish the guilty. When thirty-six civilians were kalashnikoved during the visit of the American president, she mailed letters to papers in Delhi to hold an inquiry rather than labeling the incident a work of Evil. When the government closed the post offices and cut off the phone lines, she had helped the locals to remain in clandestine contact with the world.

"Welcome to our residence, Captain Faiz!"

The two men shook hands firmly.

"Delighted… sir."

"This is Mrs. Arora!"

Captain Faiz tried folding his hands by way of a greeting.

"It must be very disappointing, Captain, to lose the war?" she asked.

He was still breathless after having climbed the trail to the colonel's house. The guards had un-handcuffed him only after stepping on the veranda.

"How I wish, madam," he said with incongruously folded hands, "I had visited you during peace time."

She was struck by his attractive looks and his impaired coordination. His sweet words, she felt, were completely unnecessary. She couldn't stop suspecting the motive behind them.

"If you think, Captain, this anti-war posturing of yours is going to melt our hearts, you are deluded."

She said the whole of it in single breath as if she had been rehearsing the line for a long time. The sharp pendants dangling from her ears resonated with the delivery.

In the prison cell, when he had been informed about the visit to the colonel's residence, he had imagined her as the catalyst behind the colonel's tendency for poetry. Now he felt she was a shell of depleted uranium. He could imagine his limbs being amputated by her words. He was at loss for words.

"Do us an honor, Captain," said the colonel. "Please sit down."

The colonel wore a blue blazer with gleaming buttons, and a poppy on the lapel.

"Whiskey?"

"With soda, sir."

The captain sat on the sofa with his knees together; he was feeling ill at ease in his clothes, which were not only tight and short, but also wrinkled and smelled of naphthalene. They were the colonel's civilian clothes from another season, ones that the orderly had delivered to the prisoner in the cell.

For a while the captain's eyes vanished in the glass case of artillery mementoes. Silver sabres. Cheetahs. Bronze knights flanking the visitors' book. Moments later, he admired the embroidery on the red-and-black Kashmiri carpet. He tried reading the many labels and cracks on every item of furniture. They captured the number of times the colonel and his wife had moved in and out of regiments.

Then suddenly the captain heard music. In the valley below, the military band was playing patriotic themes, celebrating the regiment's Raising Day. The Kargil victory had peppered the music with extra jubilation. Black-and-red tasselled sashes and tartan skirts played bagpipes and snared the drums, marching through the colonial origins of one of the largest armies in the world.

The band breezed in through the window and mixed with Colonel Arora's thoughts. During that vulnerable moment, he could have revealed all the classified information stored within him, but he did not. The GOC of his victorious regiment was involved in hushed-up scams and scandals, the latest one being the *coffin scam*. The general had bought hundreds of aluminum coffins from an American company, the coffins priced at two hundred dollars apiece. He had charged the army ten times higher. More dead Indians at the front meant more profits. Profits for the GOC and his politico friends in Delhi.

Equally touched by the music, Captain Faiz found it difficult to prolong silence about the biggest scam in his own country. He almost revealed how much the people of Pakistan *loved* their psychopathic generals—the creatures who had perfected the fine art of perpetual dictatorship.

Poetry was the safest topic to begin with and that is how everything began.

"Do you know," asked the colonel, "the meaning of our favorite poet's name?"

The military music was still churning the blood in his legs, he felt he was marching beside the bagpipes.

"Yes, sir," said the captain. "Shahid means *beloved* in our language and *martyr* in yours."

...where the year
has four, clear seasons, my mother
spoke of her childhood
...but never told me if she
also burned sticks
of jasmine...
She only
said: The monsoons never cross
the mountains into Kashmir.

It was then the boys appeared. Arjun, the colonel's son, and his friend Adi entered the room briskly. The colonel was looking forward to a fine session on poetry over the meal, specially prepared for Captain Faiz. But the boys were not interested in poetry at all. Only in interruption of poetry.

Arjun asked his mother why the house was surrounded by troops.

"They are here for a reason," said Mrs. Arora.

"That bloody custard, the GOC" said the colonel, "he has sent a whole platoon to keep an eye."

Ever since his child had reached impressionable age, the colonel had practiced self-censorship. *Custard* was the euphemism for *Bastard*.

When the boys asked if they could eat mutton, too, the colonel said, "We are vegetarians." They had become vegetarians after the doctor's report on the structure of his heart. When the children persisted, he said, "Meat is for Captain Uncle only."

The orderly had prepared meat for the guest following special instructions from a Muslim troop in the regiment. "Even if you were allowed to eat non-veg," elaborated the colonel, "you could only eat Jhatka, and not Halal."

"*We want meat! Me-eat!*"

Halal was hard to explain. Fearing they might spin him into the obscure discussion on the killing of animals, he decided to take action. "Take the kids to the lake for a swim," he ordered the orderly. "This is their punishment."

Captain Faiz laughed, floating on the sofa, watching the boys dive into their swimming costumes.

"Sir," he said staring at his whiskey. "I never had a childhood."

"Same story," said the colonel, "neither did I."

Mrs. Arora wanted to say something, but the Pakistani made them listen to his long monologue.

"I too was a lanky little boy when I was their age," said the captain in a subdued tone. "But then everything changed. One morning my mother woke me up very early. It must have been four, four-thirty. 'Father would like to see you,' she said. My head sank back to the pillow, but her voice reclaimed me. She combed my hair and wiped my face and left me in the living room, alone, with my six-foot-tall father, in military uniform. 'Young man,' said Father, 'please sit down.' Rubbing my eyes I sat down on the edge of the dining chair. Through the window I could see nothing, but the thick fog—"

"Could I," said the colonel, "complete the story."

"But sir," said the captain leaning forward.

"Then the orderly," continued the colonel, "served us tea from a trembling tray. Father looked at me for a long time. 'Young man,' he said, 'I am leaving for Kashmir.' Still quite drowsy, I downed the warm cup of tea and asked, 'Will you live in the houseboat,

Papa?' Papa was silent for a while. 'Young man,' he said, 'I may not return.' Then my mother's brothers arrived in a military jeep. They were leaving, too, for the same war. Papa hugged me, then hugged Mother, that was the only time he hugged Mother in public. Before the jeep disappeared in the fog, Papa bowed his head before me and waved his inspection stick as if apologizing for having failed me."

A long silence followed; it chilled the entire house.

"Colonel-sahib, how do you know such details from my life?" asked Captain Faiz.

"Our Intelligence," interjected the hostess, "is a disaster. It is the courage of jawans and officers that keeps us going."

"Colonel-sahib, have you always worked for Indian Intelligence?" asked Captain Faiz.

"Young man," said the colonel with sweat on the forehead, "I know the story because it is also my story."

The regiment band was silent, no longer sending in gusts of bagpipes through the windows. Simrita Arora noticed the two men staring, one at the other.

"Even I didn't know this," she said. "Why didn't you tell me before?" She spoke so inaudibly that the colonel had to lean to catch her words.

"Be... Because..." The colonel lapsed into incoherence. Simrita Arora turned to Captain Faiz.

"Did your father return?" she almost whispered while offering him a bowl of apples.

"Madam, not a single day has gone by when he didn't return."

They could not eat the meal.

When he left she returned his greeting with folded hands. For a long time afterwards she was curious about the enemy soldier; perhaps that is why she was determined to keep her curiosity hidden. The colonel perceived it with crushing clarity.

"Good night," he said and departed to his bedroom.

Before sleep took over, she hummed the Sufi songs and examined the reasons why their lives had taken such a sad turn.

It is pain
from which love departs into all new pain:
Freedom's terrible thirst, flooding Kashmir,
is bringing love to its tormented glass.
Stranger, who will inherit the last night
of the past? Of whom shall I not sing, and sing?

Next morning, the GOC evinced enormous curiosity during his meeting with the colonel.

"Is poetry of any use?" he asked. "Have we unmasked the enemy?"

"Nothing has surfaced yet, sir," said the colonel. "But we have established considerable trust."

"That is not enough," said the GOC harshly.

"Sir, taking the prisoner to my house," reminded the colonel, "was doing more than enough."

"You will take him home again."

"A second visit?"

"And if we don't see *results* this time, we'll interrogate the chap physically. The future of our country is at stake."

"But, sir," said the colonel, "Faiz is our prize catch. His rank is that of a captain. We could use him to bargain with the Pakistanis. For him they might release at least ten of our own lower-ranking boys."

"We know this," said the GOC. "That is why this is your last chance."

The colonel pacified the GOC with assurances of a *breakthrough* and marched back to his office to make arrangements.

Later in the evening, when Captain Faiz was un-handcuffed by the guards on the veranda, he knew he was entering a safe place.

When he greeted her with folded hands, a smile fermented on Simrita Arora's face, and he knew from now on there would be no need to brace himself. Even her tone had changed, softened. Her gestures had diminished somewhat. And yet he couldn't stop stammering a bit, just like during the previous visit.

After the meal, they stood out in the veranda and watched the distant film in the valley below.

The heroine was about to be martyred for falling in love with the prince. Bricks were inching up around the beautiful woman. The colonel and his wife and the captain stood silently as they watched the film from a distance. The guards were still as well, gawking at the spectacle. Their shadows stirring like moths.

"Colonel-sahib, is it a silent film?"

"Sound is blocked by the hill. Look over there. Tiger Hill. Would you like to watch the film?"

"No. No... Yessir."

"Good," said the colonel, "this experience is not to be missed."

"Sir."

"My wife will accompany you," said the colonel.

"I, I, didn't hear you, sir."

"I said my wife *will* accompany you."

Simrita Arora was not startled by the colonel's words. She seemed in a strange agreement with her husband, one that the captain suspected, but did not probe. He warned himself against jumping to conclusions.

While the colonel engaged the soldiers in conversation, Captain Faiz and Simrita Arora departed through the rear entrance. On the colonel's instructions they rode the artillery mules; it was too long a walk otherwise. Before waving them off, the colonel, for the first time, asked Captain Faiz to give his word as an officer that he would not escape.

She guided the mule gently on the tracks. He followed. Darkness was spreading quickly, the wind had already maddened the pines, and the valley below was shimmering with little dots of light. The bells on his mule's harness jingled as he followed her all the way to the Iron-Age chalk figures, which were etched on the hillside, and were phosphorescent on that night.

"The film is called *Mughal-e-Azam*," she said.

They sat on the naked roots of a solitary pine tree, watching. The roots barely clutched the lime soil beneath them. The sound of insects crackled, mingling with the soundtrack of the film.

The prince shot an arrow and unveiled the statue of a woman in the garden. There was applause. Courtiers. Common folk. Royalty. The prince's apprenticeship was over—he was ready to replace his father on the throne. There were tears in the queen's eyes, but the king dragged her back to the palace. When the prince was alone in the garden, the marble statue walked toward the fountain. "Wait," said the prince. "Why didn't you protest when I shot the arrow,? It could have killed you" The statue woman, whose name was Anarkali, laughed hysterically. "I wanted to see, Your Highness, how a fiction transforms into reality."

Anarkali's voice filled Captain Faiz with hope; it was like reading Shahid.

They followed a different mule track on the way back. She dismounted by the chalk figures, and pointed at their veranda on the mountain across from them. The lights were on and the moths were buzzing about. The moths are soldiers, she clarified.

"Over there," she said, "Pakistan is on the other side of these hills."

"I know," he said.

"Go," she said. "Now."

"No." He spoke as if his mind was made up.

"If you stay, they will torture you."

"If I go, they will court martial Colonel-sahib."

"We have lived our life," she said.

"No."

"Both of us want you to go," she said. "But if you *do* go, I will win the bet. If you stay, he will."

"For them," he stammered, "I am a disgrace."

"What do you mean?"

"Madam, I don't want to go."

"GO," she said. "This is not a film."

"Madam, my commanders..."

"Complete it," she said, "complete the sentence."

"My commanders wanted to kill me."

"You're lying to me?"

"Promise me," he said, "not a word of this to Colonel-sahib." She shook her head.

"Madam, my commanders didn't receive the ammunition on time, and yet they didn't delay the attack. The casualty rate was bound to be ninety percent, madam, and yet in their guts *attacking* made sense... We all begged them, we begged them to come back to their senses. They gave us each a big bottle of rum. If you return back alive, they told us, rum will be charged onto your account."

"I will never go back," he stammered. "Ne-ver."

She held him. She was wearing nothing underneath, noticed Captain Faiz, indeed she was wearing nothing except the light film of her pheran. Then he couldn't see anything at all. Blackness descended on them from the mountains and they moved into one another's arms. When they emerged she had tears gleaming on her face.

The captain attempted again to commit to memory the warmth of her hands. But he couldn't. She was still. Her silence was not really silent like many of her words. Her silence was killing him.

Nothing survived. Perhaps a glint of transgression.

She lay for a long time on him, the way warm snow lies on transparent trees in the winter and buckles them. She probed the shrapnel in his elbow with her fingers. He hid his face in her breasts. The mountains moved, also the lime beneath them.

"What are you thinking?" he asked, touching the curve of her throat.

"Thinking, how people loved each other during the time of the Sufis." And she asked him, "Who is in Pakistan?"

"M... mother."

"How old is she?"

"She does not remember me. When I meet her there are tears in her eyes. But she has no idea—"

"Sorry."

"Protect yourself," he said. "My commanders are planning a new assault. Hundreds of soldiers will infiltrate Kashmir, disguised as freedom fighters. They will suicide bomb the army camps—"

"That's enough," she said. "This information will save my husband."

They returned through the back entrance, an hour before daybreak, smeared with lime, smelling of pine resin. She received assistance from a village woman to pull his mule. He was feeling very weak. On the tracks he had muttered the name of a woman many times, perhaps his mother.

"The children are asleep," whispered the colonel. "How was the film?"

"Forget the film," she said. "The captain needs rest."

"He is going back to the cell."

"Did you forget we are hosting him? Did you forget Indian hospitality?"

The colonel disregarded the GOC's orders and helped move the guest to his wife's bedroom. They didn't say a word to each other in the living room. She was about to lie on the sofa when he put his arm around her shoulders and touched the flash in her hair and walked her to his bed.

"Are you happy?" he asked her, wiping the lime from her face.

"I lost the bet," she said.

"How long will the happiness last?" he asked, tickling her back.

"Six months," she said. "Stop it. What are you doing?"

"Nothing," said the colonel. "Make sure it lasts for a long time."

She nodded. He nodded. His breath was so heavy it moved the greying hair on his chest. He ignored the demands of his weak heart and covered her body with kisses and bites and bruises. No one heard them out beyond the curtains.

After the coffins, men were exchanged at the border. On December 11, three days after Shahid died of a brain tumour in America, the two armies at the Indo-Pak border installed three white flags on a hilltop and declared a temporary ceasefire. Captain Faiz and five of his men were exchanged for eleven Indian captives. The Pakistani Army had tortured the youth out of every Indian soldier. The corpses had been cut up.

Just before he left, Captain Faiz turned to them. It was as if someone had painted water colors on his face. He looked horrible.

"Madam," he said handing her the ream of poems, "they are for both of you."

She could have flashed a smile, but refrained, and slowly turned to her husband.

"No," protested the colonel, "these are your poems. Keep

them."

"Colonel-sahib," he said. "Poetry belongs to those for whom it is written."

The colonel ordered the guards to return Shahid back to the captain. The enemy accepted the book, clicked his heels and saluted as if he was in front of a senior officer in his own army.

"Dis-miss," said the colonel.

> Yes, I remember it,
> The day I'll die, I broadcast the crimson,
>
> so long ago of that sky, its spread air,
> its rushing dyes, and a piece of earth
>
> bleeding, apart from the shore, as we went,
> on the day I'll die, past the guards, and he,
>
> keeper of the world's last saffron, rowed me
> on an island the size of a grave.

From the observation deck the colonel and his wife watched their guest sink into the valley, completely oblivious to the icy wind and the guard's finger pointing at the peaks where the enemy posts were. As time passed, the figure changed into a sapling, moving up and down the slopes. Slowly the sapling diminished into an impressionist's strand of hair and crossed the flimsy foot-bridge over the river. Only a dot, or perhaps a cloud of vapor, the vapor slipping further and further into the land beyond reach.

≈

Student of Gardens

This is the youngest of all. This is the Garden of Beginnings, designed by Queen Noor Jahen. Here on this octagonal rock she met Emperor Jahengir, the world seizer. There under the reddened chenar tree, she kissed the Emperor's hand. There she invented the attar-of-roses. Here she rubbed a drop on the palm of her hand— and it seemed as if whole battalions of roses bloomed. Many hearts were revived. Many souls unwithered. "This," she declared, "is the foretaste of Paradise."

It was the Sikh boy, the Sikh boy in the class who fully comprehended Ms. Rubaiya's lessons.

During recess he walked to her desk. "Teacher-sahiba," he said, "your lesson is very relevant."

"Why so?"

"Because *this* is a city of gardens."

"Oh," she said, "and I thought *this* was just an army camp."

"Don't be deceived by the jumpy soldiers," he said.

Scepticism flared in her face, but she followed his pointed finger. The slopes of the mountains were lined with gardens. The Garden of Morning Breezes stood next to the sprawling Garden of Heart's Ease. The Garden of Fidelity stood entangled with the Garden of Involuntary Memories. The Garden of Telegraph

Flowers—sumptuous and delicate, its terraces running in and out of the tree line. The Garden of Four Oracles bound by the Garden of Two Exactitudes and the Garden of Invisible Gondolas. On the spur of the tallest mountain, overlooking the lake, swayed the Garden of Latticed Light, before the Garden of Ice Lingam, and after the Garden of Joy of Water.

"The soldiers," explained the boy, "are here to guard the gardens from the civilians."

Ms. Rubaiya remembered the first day she had arrived in the city. It was supposed to be a brief vacation at her distant brother Major Manto's house, after losing her job.

"Stay longer," her brother ordered. "In this place there are many students without a teacher, and you are a teacher without students."

"Where is the school?"

"Used to be in a tent, but now it is in a tank garage."

"I will stay for a month only."

Perhaps it was she who needed the boys more than they needed her. All of them? No, only that one, the long-haired boy. He opened her eyes to the gardens. She was no longer blind. Because of him she was able to hear the fountains of water inside the gardens. She was no longer deaf. Every Tuesday, after school, she would spread a bedsheet on the lawn by the barracks, listen to the military bagpipes, and hold a small session with him.

"Stay longer," the boy insisted.

"Why?"

"Because *this* is the city of gardens. And your brother, the commander of the soldiers, is *actually* a custodian of gardens."

"What use are the gardens," she asked, "if people cannot visit them?"

"Teacher-sahiba," he whispered, "people forget how to *be* in the gardens. The soldiers are helping us realize the importance of gardens."

She stayed.

This is the oldest of all. This is the Garden of Unanswered Questions. This one rises like a wave from the hill of cypresses. Here in AD *1617, Emperor Jehangir tried to speculate the distance to heaven (from earth) in a poem he composed for his Queen, Noor Jehan. Here, on this pavilion by the slender fountain, the Emperor digressed and grew curious about the properties of visible and invisible wavelengths. How long does it take for light to travel between a King's earlobe and shoulder? That night, while making love, he mumbled many rough estimates, especially when his Queen probed about the expansion of empires and limits of motion. Yes. This is the Garden of Visions and Revisions.*

The new surroundings, clean and fresh air, inspired Ms. Rubaiya to deliver lectures on history and botany, subjects long overlooked. Hardly a week after joining, she marched her students away from the tank shelter to the nearest garden.

"KEEP AWAY," warned the sign on the metal fence.

She sat under a spreading chenar tree outside the garden. The pupils sat in a semi-circle around her, confused and delighted by her sleeveless blouse, dusky yellow sari, and smooth feet comfortably embedded in filigree sandals.

"You." She asked the Sikh boy to the front. He spoke from his memory the things he knew—how red poppies had melted into shoots of irises two seasons ago.

"Class," she said patting the boy on his back, "from tomorrow this boy will be your monitor, and from tomorrow you'll follow the new timetable."

The Garden of Dizzying Geometry—on Monday.

The Garden of Temporary Fluids—on Tuesday.

The Garden of Whispered Music—on Wednesday.

(No class on Thursday. Cricket)

The Garden of Edible Roses—on Friday.

The soldiers outside the garden were astonished by her unconventional methods. They gazed at the class through binoculars from raised posts by the fence. Sometimes fingers of smoke from the distant civilian quarters blocked the lenses. Only then they rested.

"What textbook should we use?" the boys asked their new teacher.

"Use books," she said, "but never the textbooks. They are full of errors and horrible mistakes. See, what a difference an *S* makes. The *Mass Slaughter of Migratory Birds* is printed wrongly as the *Mass Laughter of Migratory Birds.*"

"Teacher-sahiba," the Sikh boy raised his hand. He was still standing in front of the class.

"Yes, you have my permission to speak."

"Teacher-sahiba," he said, "see what a difference a *T* makes. The word *Error* is printed wrongly as *Terror.*"

On Tuesday she met the boy, alone, after the class, by a captured Pakistani tank. She told him things about the nineteenth century. The gardens were open to the civilians then. She told him about the people of that period, about young Victor Jacquement, the French botanist, who visited Queen Noor Jahen's garden in AD 1831.

"You mean," the boy pointed his hand, "that garden with a carpet of blue-bell flowers?"

"No," she said turning, "that one, the one swaying by the gondolas."

She did not tell the boy about the letters the Frenchman wrote back home to a friend. She avoided things that normally got in the way. "In Kashmir, my friend, I find it difficult to disrobe and make love until I have satisfactorily explained to my beloved Kepler's laws of planetary motion." Why Kepler's laws? she

73

thought. Why not Mendel? Why didn't the Frenchman whisper those Latinized botanical names in the ears of his lovers? Were they paid women? Teacher-sahiba did not know.

"Why did the botanist visit Kashmir?" asked the boy. "Don't they have gardens in France?"

"They do. Big ones. But ours are better."

She loaned him a *safe* book to read from that period.

"Any mistakes in this one, Teacher-sahiba?"

"Not any more. I corrected them all."

She found it hard to correct her own mistakes. Was the Sikh boy perhaps her biggest mistake of all? He aired the red embers burning her heart. He was turning her whole body into a garden, and the garden into ashes. Soon the embroidered magnolias on her sari would be charred. Nothing was safe.

"But why," she thought on returning back home, "Why do we fall for people who are not our type. Why is the boy so very young, younger than the universe? He wears shorts, he is almost a baby."

"You should be ashamed of yourself," said Major Manto during the meal.

"But, Brother, do you know how much the boy means to me? Do you?"

"The boy's *age* gets in the way."

"Yes, Brother."

Major Manto stepped out of the house with a double-barrelled gun. He followed the cobbled trail that led all the way to the Garden of Hermit's Tresses. Not long ago he had aimed at two civilian stalkers, wounding one in the foot. They had set fire to a wooden fence. On the morning after the shooting, the yellow field of flowers next the gutted fence had turned red.

Alone in the house she re-read the letter from the boy.

Dear Teacher-sahiba,

I have decided. I would like to live with you. This way I will learn more and better. I disagree with you when you say, "Age is a border that cannot be crossed." I have thought of a permanent solution to this problem. From today I will grow old faster.

Love,

Adi Singh. (Roll No. 12)

She heaved a sigh of relief when her brother returned to the house that night without discharging his gun. She folded the letter and hid it in her bosom.

On Tuesday, the boy showed her the Garden of Hundred-leaved Lightness, the Garden of Good Streams, the Garden of Eight Paradises, the Garden of Chiselled Stillness, the Garden of Fluted Stones, the Garden of Enlightened Expectations, the Garden of Za-fran, the Garden of Excavated Colors, and the Garden of Going No Further. She kissed him on the forehead. They held hands watching the sheep graze in the meadows.

She pointed at the sheer cliff. "Look, on top is the Blessed Garden of Prophet's Hair. And next to it is the Garden of Fairies, and beside it the Garden of Issa Christ."

"That must be a misprint, Teacher-sahiba," said the boy. "Issa never visited the City of Gardens."

"They say," she said, "Issa survived the crucifixion and migrated here. He lived until the ripe age of 112. His garden is also known as the Garden of Shepherd's Love. One day I will walk you to his tomb."

"Teacher-sahiba," he asked, "what is that mathematical sign doing in the garden?"

"Cross, you mean," she said.

"Yes," he said, "the Plus sign."

Ms. Rubaiya and the boy felt a deep peace learning from each other, pointing at things. The peace left them the moment they spotted the major inside the Garden of Embraces. Every Tuesday, between 0700 hrs and 1800 hrs, the major supervised the garden soldiers.

"Sister, what did you cover in the class today?" asked Major Manto as he approached them. He stood very close to his side of the fence.

"What does this man know about *covering*?" she said to herself. "Teaching is *discovering*, not covering."

"What did you cover?"

"Long ago a botanist enriched his collection of plants by more than 600 items in this city. He gathered a currant bush (*Ribes alpestre*), some nettle trees (*Celtis sinensis*), wild pears (*Pyrus indicus*), alders (*Alnus nitida*), eunymus, azaleas, jasmines, anemones, aquilegias, euphorbias, and quantities of rhododendrons. I told the boy—"

"How many pupils are there in your class?"

"Thirteen."

"But you talk as if there is only ONE? This one."

Major Manto looked down at the boy, who was chalking some long words on the fence.

"You are a bad example," he said, raising his voice. "Why don't you go play with other boys?"

"Let's invite him home for food," said Ms. Rubaiya.

"You should be ashamed of yourself, Sister," said the major.

"Leave him alone. I beg you."

That evening when the boy met her again by the barracks she asked him politely, "Go away."

"Such things have happened before," he said. "Boys. Women."

"It is unhealthy," she said. "Plus, I don't believe you are my type."

"Difference is good," he said.

"Your age gets in the way, my brother says."

"I am trying hard to grow old faster."

"So you say," she said, gazing at the undulations of an unfamiliar garden. "Age is a border—"

"Don't be afraid of age," he said. "Age is repetition, nothing more."

"Wrong. Age is waiting. Even Emperors had to wait."

This is the Garden of Smallest Divisions of Time. Here in the seventeenth century Prince Salim saw the beautiful Mehr-un-Nisa for one brief moment, and forever lost his heart. Mehr-un-Nisa was the daughter of exiled Persians. Here in this garden Salim entertained the idea to gift her a rose. But—here Prince Salim's father, the Emperor, too, noticed Mehr-un-Nisa and quickly got her married to one of his generals. Here Salim had to wait until he ascended the throne. This is where Salim waited until people began calling him Emperor Jehangir, the world-seizer, and until Mehr-un-Nisa became a widow. Here he waited for four more years until she had fully mourned her dead husband and until she received a nod from her brother. Then, as a perfectly mature man, he, the Emperor (with 300 women waiting in the harem), extended his hand to her. She, who had just turned thirty-four, kissed the hand by way of a perfectly mature answer. Here, among the slender columns, he gave her the title of Noor Jahen, the sea of light. Here he declared that all good things had migrated from Persia to India to him. The chenar trees had migrated. So had his Queen —the tree of joy and happiness.

"I have recently revised my ideas about love," the Emperor wrote in his diary. "Before I married Noor Jahen, I never knew what love was. The laws of love and the laws of happiness and the laws of pain are identical."

Then suddenly the boy revised his age. Ms. Rubaiya was not ready. It was a Tuesday. She was sitting on a chair on the cobbled yard outside the house and had just finished telling her brother about the difficult test she had handed out to her class. In her hands was a book on Afghan flowers.

The boy arrived on his red bicycle, smelling of wild flowers.

"Poppies?" she asked herself. What do poppies stand for? Remembrance? Forgetting? Sometimes symbols get in the way, she thought. He stood before the metallic gate. The suddenness of the event astonished her.

"Permission to enter?" he asked.

"Yes, yes, you don't need permission," she said and waved at the sentry to allow the boy in.

"Please listen. I am much older, Teacher-sahiba. Only a month younger than you."

"Certainly you have grown older," she said kissing his hand. "And you have become a beautiful liar. But, your age still gets in the way."

"I am so sorry."

"Wait," she said. "Where are you going?"

He slipped away peddling his bicycle. Slipped away like a sad breeze back to the space between the gardens. She touched the corners of her eyes lightly.

"Still, there is reason for optimism," she told Major Manto.

"Rubaiya, the boy's age gets in the way. I beg you."

Major Brother raised his voice.

"God, the expressions he makes," she said to herself.

Major Manto meant well. He was planning to quit the military job to help her hunt for a proper husband. He desired his distant sister to marry a man who could guard her for life. "Not one of those third-class boys everready to run away from the first wrinkle on a woman's face."

On Tuesday the Major drove to the HQ.

"I've done enough for this godforsaken country," he announced to the regiment god, the General Officer Commanding.

"Your biggest achievement," said the GOC, "is ahead of you."

"Sir, I have defended every inch of our land. Defended the Garden of Frozen Turbulence, the Garden of Medieval Flowers, the Garden of Distinguished Follies, the Garden of Forking Paths, the Garden of a Humble Administrator. It's time young blood gets the chance. People like me ought to retire."

Permission was not granted.

"What will become of me if the boy fails the test," thought Ms. Rubaiya. She locked herself in the bathroom. She caressed her skin with oil of almonds and rubbed away the cracks on the soles of her feet with salted pine needles. What she could not rub away was her love for the boy. It terrified her. She felt she was dying for him. The softness of her skin, the precision of her ample curves, everything was dying.

"You take long baths," said brother Manto tapping on the door. "Like civilians. Almost like women."

"I *am* a woman," she clarified. "And why are the civilians not allowed in the gardens?"

"They have poor eyesight," he said.

After the bath, she used indigo ink to cover her breasts with words—*Ribes alpestre, Celtis sinensis, Pyrus indicus, Sorbus nepalenensis, Alnus nitida....*

"Hurry up," announced Manto on the tenth knock, which almost unbolted the door. "Otherwise how will I know if you are still alive?"

"Yes, Brother."

She felt she must not get in his way. She felt she must die. Die like the dead language on her breasts, then re-emerge as the name of a flower. What is death? Death is a garden.

This is the Garden of Solitude. This is the Garden of Perished Memories. This is the Garden of Partings. The Garden of Designed Minimalism. Queen Noor Jahen composed her own epitaph here on this sheer cliff:

> *Upon my grave when I shall die,*
> *No lamp shall burn nor jasmine lie,*
> *No candle, with unsteady flame,*
> *Serve as reminder of my fame,*
> *No bulbul chanting overhead,*
> *Shall tell the world that I am dead.*

Major Manto held the boy's ears and raised him up in the air. "How much did you see through the ventilator?" he probed with embarrassment. The boy remained silent, incomprehension floating on his face.

As the major dropped the boy on the ground, the boy muttered Latin names, the ones he had seen on Ms. Rubaiya's breasts. He had used a drum to become tall, almost as tall as the poplars lining the lawn, taller than the tinned roof over the bathroom.

"What exactly did you see?"

"I saw fruits," said the boy without hesitation. "I saw twins. Beautiful twins. They inspired me to do an experiment."

"What?" boomed the major.

The boy walked to the table in the corner, dug out a fountain pen from his pocket. His hand shook mildly as he dropped a large drop of ink on the table. Then he dropped another drop, equally large, on top of the first drop and said, "See, sir, one plus one equals one."

Major Manto's eyes sent a bolt of lightening toward him.

Major Manto's garden-soldiers arrested the boy.

"Take him to the wretched Garden of Issa Christ," he instructed, "and tie him to the cross."

The soldiers marched the boy to the sheer cliff. A trail of schoolboys marched behind him, staring with fear. The civilians peered out of their windows. The guards on the raised posts gazed at the tableau through binoculars until the boy's hands and feet were tied with ropes to the cross. Only when the onlookers left, the boy felt a movement in the ground beneath. He looked down. In the valley the Garden of Chaste Memories was stretching toward him. The Garden of Hours was dreaming of him. The Garden of Two Sisters was glowing for him. The Garden of Gabbehs was melting because of him. But he felt nothing. No emotion.

This is the Unfinished Garden, the Garden of Hope. Here Queen Noor Jahen's father-in-law, Emperor Akbar, rested after conquering Kashmir in AD 1586. Here he dictated the following words: "The sole idea of the wise kings is day by day to refresh the garden of the world by the streams of justice." Here he planted 1,000 chenars by the lake waters. Here the Queen was vexed by a boatman, the one who uprooted a beautiful chenar tree. Here Emperor Akbar's son ordered a courtier to cut off the boatman's thumbs as a warning to others.

The boat people were the first to see a sheath of light originating from the sheer cliff. They could see from far, far away, the light as they steered their delicate boats to the city of gardens. On touching the edge of the lake they lifted their ragged cloaks and rushed with fish sacks to their mud and straw houses. That night children inserted fingers in their ears. Never before had they witnessed a thunder so intense. Then there was rain. Water danced on tin roofs. Because the windows were shrouded with tarpaulin, the children could not notice the little landslides in the Garden of Issa Christ, or the precise time when the cross tore itself from the cliff.

During his fall the boy saw Heaven. God blew wet breath on his cheeks. The well-oiled knot of hair on his head uncoiled, and somersaulted a little ahead of him. He stopped beating his wings, paused in mid-air to get a good view of the valley, then looked up.

"Careful," said the Angel, "you might collide with the edge of a cloud." The boy said nothing, he was startled by the Angel's speed. She swam to him, faster than light, from a crevice in the sheer cliff. "Look," she continued, "look at the arc of the gardens down there." The boy looked at the Angel. She resembled Queen Noor Jahen. He had seen her pictures in many, many borrowed books. "Once upon a time," she said, "an emperor declared—If I were to die, I would like to take my gardens along."

"I have lost faith," said the boy as he was falling. "I no longer believe in gardens."

"Only people without imagination lose faith," she said leaping toward him.

"What use are the gardens," said the boy, "if I can not live with Teacher-sahiba?"

"You cannot accomplish love in a single day," she said. "Love is a garden. Didn't you hear the Persian song of songs?"

> *i plant my hands in the small garden:*
> *i will grow green.*
> *i know, i know, i know.*
>
> *and the birds*
> *will lay eggs*
> *in the grooves*
> *of my inky fingers*

A warm current from the South swung him like a pendulum over the border. He swayed this way and that, above the fuzzy line, unable to choose. The wind strummed the barbed wire, leaving both sides of the border with beautiful music. Beautiful and unprecedented. The Angel's eyelids were full of tears.

Crash.

"You killed the boy," said Ms. Rubaiya.

"Don't be ridiculous," protested the major. "Being a woman, you are emotional. I just wanted to make the boy tough."

"You are responsible," said Ms. Rubaiya. "I am leaving."

"Stay," requested the major. He alerted all the 587 border posts. The garden soldiers and the border soldiers launched massive search operations despite the fog. By midnight the major had his answer. He woke his sister from deep sleep and announced, "Nothing is ruined, everything is in control." Word by word, he conveyed to her the radio operator's dispatch. A message had arrived from the enemy territory: *Adi found alive on our side of the border.*

Time passed. One day the expected letter arrived.

Dear Teacher-sahiba,

I think of you often, but today I thought of you all day because it is a special occasion. Happy Birthday! Why didn't you visit me in the hospital? Are you angry with me?

I have already forgiven your brother. I forgave him the day I returned from the other side of the border (They were good to me, the enemy uncles and aunts).

After the fall, I have become older and wiser, Teacher-sahiba. I think my punishment was actually my reward.

You won't believe, you won't believe your eyes when you see me.

So much I have changed. I look at the mirror and say it is a different person. But one thing has not changed. My love for you keeps growing.

My plaster was removed two days ago and tomorrow I will be able to ride the new Harley motorcycle my uncle bought for me. So much I am looking forward to taking you out on the Harley to see the gardens, which we have yet to discover because they are far from our city. Please would you come along, Teacher-sahiba? Every Tuesday I will wait under your window until you come down in the yard.

I love you,

Adi Singh.

PS: Pl also find in the envelope the list of gardens we have yet to visit. Topmost on the list are: The Garden of Unreal Estate, the Garden of Miniature Sublime, and the Garden of Unfolding Proposals.

"Don't!" she felt like screaming when she saw him headed to the house on his Harley. He parked the noisy machine. He didn't ask for permission to enter and took the flight of stairs to her room. She was combing her hair.

"You were going to wait under the window," she said harshly, contradicting the rush of tenderness within her.

"Plan B has been implemented," he said flinging open his arms.

"Plan B?"

"Teacher-sahiba," he said with brand-new confidence in his voice, "I have grown very wise."

Saying this he raised his toes, lifted himself, and their burning lips joined. Then, again.

Again.

"Very bad," she mumbled squeezing his hands. "We shouldn't have."

But, it was a little too late.

"Your lips," he declared, "taste like salt tea."

"And yours are smelly," she replied, "like the rose attar."

He smiled. She smiled. They felt they could grow their two smiles into a garden.

Outside, Major Manto was watering the poppies in square plots at the edge of the cobbled yard. Poppies—Forgetting. Remembering? Nothing was clear. Ms. Rubaiya and the boy stepped out. The boy started the machine.

The major wiped his hands on his khakhi trousers. He handed his sister a darkening poppy. "Stay," he said forcefully. "Please reconsider. If you stay, we will open the gates to 954 gardens. We will allow the civilians in. We won't shoot them even if they visit the garden of their choice. We won't fire even if they start making victory signs."

"My mind is made up," she insisted.

"Your mind is *not* made up," he said clamping her arm tightly.

"The boy is waiting."

"There are boys waiting for you in the school."

Her eyes welled up. She resisted them. "Tears," she said, "are not an efficient way to express emotion. Total waste of salt."

This is the Garden of Becoming Lighter than Air. This is the Garden of Shapes of Water. Matter is transformed here by the geometry of patterns, by many mosaics of abstraction. Here stone loses solidity. Heaviness of jasper and marble disappears somewhere in the limitless gush of the channels. And one blows freely through the interstices of color, and one stirs the Head Gardener's apparatus. This is the Garden of Imagination. This is the Garden of Showering your Beloved with Gifts. Here Queen Noor Jahen's son arrived in a procession of 500 elephants. Here he conceived the idea of building a monument for Queen Noor Jahen's niece, Mumtaj. Here lies the Garden of Pure Love. Here lies the germ of the Taj.

Lessons resumed in the tank garage.

The substitute teacher, with a dewy smile on her cheek, started an unfinished chapter, the one not covered by Ms. Rubaiya. She was particularly impressed by one boy's knowledge of the gardens, which didn't match the textbook, but did manage to touch her heart. She asked him to stand in front of the class and speak from memory the things he knew.

The boy spoke, pointing his finger toward the Garden of Outdoor Rooms, the Garden of Eroded Brightness, the Garden of the Pain of a Dervish, the Garden of Unrequited Flowers, the Garden of an Unsuccessful Soldier.

"And over there," he said, "is the endlessly lonely Garden of Fidelity."

~

Tiger

Last June, General Manto was driving back home through the mountain roads when his jeep broke down. He stepped out in the dark. Not a single vehicle passed by for a long time. Finally, a family of peasants noticed him. They stepped out of their deodar huts and pushed the dead jeep to the shoulder. One of them mentioned the distant landslides and roadblocks. Another offered food. "No, thank you," said the general. "I can not stomach your rustic preparations. You people add gallons of ghee. One day you all will die of ghee."

General Manto covered the remaining seven-and-a-half miles on foot. He walked by the River Chenab and arrived at the army camp in less than three hours. By the time he swaggered into his house, his medal-heavy uniform was saturated with mud and he could smell his own sweat. All the house lights were on. "What is the use of turning them on," he muttered. "She doesn't live here any more."

General Manto, the GOC of the armoured corps, was short, but very athletic, with a handlebar moustache. The left side of his face was covered with little marks of smallpox. The right side was unusually smooth. Both sides had flared with confidence and authority when the Defence Minister had decorated him with a double medal exactly a year ago.

"Bring me a scotch," General Manto ordered loudly.

Mundu didn't answer.

The general stripped out of his uniform and dashed to the bathroom and urgently peed in the commode.

"Ramji, bring me a relaxing chair on the veranda, samajhliya," he thundered while wetting the rim of the commode.

Still no answer.

"Mundu, Ramji, oyeh, where to vanish?" he yelled again while taking his shower. "You bloody sons-of-an-owl. I'll order my major to lock you in the POW camp."

Mundu and Ramji shared a parrot-green canvas tent as their sleeping quarters, pitched fifty yards from the house, separated by a large garden with three lines of red poppies. The two men were playing cards and slurping very sweet tea the moment the grandee barged into the house. They were listening to old Lata Mageshkar songs on All India Radio. Two candles, placed on a black aluminum trunk, filled the tent with festive light. Mundu, the younger of the two, was the new orderly; Ramji was sahib's old-time chef.

General Manto rolled up the side flap of the tent.

The new orderly's hands acquired a nervous lubricity, his cards landed inside warm tea.

"General-sahib, Gen-sahib..." he leaped up. Stiff, mildly quivering.

Sahib didn't shut off the flashlight, he just cleared his throat. The cone of light fell on yellowing Bollywood magazines next to Mundu's polar sleeping bag.

"Sir, we waited for long, sir. Called the Radio Operator, sir, but he said, sir—"

Sahib cleared his throat, raised his brow and flashed the cone of light on Mundu's muddy brown canvas shoes.

"Sir, the Morse code said, sir, that *Tiger departing Charlie-*

Romeo at 0800 hours, sir."

"Idiot! My jeep broke down. Tiger is back home."

"Sir."

"Bring me a scotch. Jaldi, fast. On the veranda. Big Patiala peg."

"Yessir."

"Ramji, you fry peanuts, crispy," he said snapping his fingers.

"Fast. Taratari. Taratari."

"Yessir."

Ramji guided nervous Mundu towards the glass cabinet. Mundu had arrived a week earlier, fresh from 3rd Regiment. He was unfamiliar with the yellow stucco house. The upper shelf brimmed with supplies from the army canteen. Hercules xxx Rum. Johnny Walker whiskey. Thunderbolt beer. The lower shelf was occupied by neat rows of thumb-sized bottles, shiny glass vials packed with homeopathic beads. White sugary pills. This shelf was strictly out of bounds, not to be touched.

General Manto settled down comfortably on the veranda. There was a slight chill in the air. The valley below was shimmering with lights from the barracks. As usual he turned on the HMV record player, the one he had received as additional dowry, two months after his wedding.

Mundu poured scotch in the glass. He added ice cubes to the drink as if he was dropping stones in the middle of a lake. Fronds of brown fluid spouted out of the glass, raced down through a crack in the table. General Manto's Light Machine Gun anger penetrated the clumsy jawan.

Mundu rushed back to the kitchen like a wounded child.

"Why doesn't he sleep?"

"Last month his wife ran away."

"Why?"

"He is ugly."

"Not all wives run away."

"Good she ran away."

"You didn't like her?"

"She kept an eye on the cabinet, locked everything."

"Did you?"

"No. Do I look like a thief?"

"Who she run away with?"

"Minister's son."

"Bakshi, the artisht!"

"Thurkee artisht!"

> *Black is black,*
> *I want my baby back.*
> *It's grey, it's grey*
> *Since she went away, oh oh*

"He is playing gitmit music," reported Mundu.

"Plays the old song all the time," replied Ramji.

"Don't get a word."

"English music goes phut-phut-phut."

"Officer people stop listening to Indian singers. Lata Mangeshkar means nothing to them."

"How long will this drama go on?"

"Late."

"We are not his servants?"

"We are militarymen…"

"Why did you join the military?"

"Country. Patriotism."

"No, the real reason?"

"Stomach."

"Stomach."

"No office tomorrow for General?"

"Generals go in whenever."

"But, he is a fake general, no?"

"Meaning?"

"Rose from the ranks?"

"Yessir."

"How come?"

"Homeopathy."

"Homeopathy?"

"General treated Defence Minister's ex-wife. She had tumor."

"Six months after he picked the rank, she died."

"Dead... Khatam."

"Khatam."

"Idiots," the general yelled for another drink. "They work slower than women. Bring taratari, taratari."

Mundu experienced a spell of vertigo, a total blackout, when he stood with a tray in front of General-sahib. A pungent aroma filled the entire veranda when the bowl of peanuts fell accidentally on sahib's navel. Manto-sahib rose from his chair and with the force of ten Shivas slapped him.

"Idiot! Haramzada."

Bruised, the new orderly turned to the kitchen.

"Where are you going? Wait. Call the Radio Operator. Tell him my jeep broke down close to the bridge. Understand?"

Manto-sahib followed the orderly to the living room. The orderly did not witness the precise moment when sahib kissed his wife's framed photo, lying next to the red phone on the cabinet. Sahib hurled the photo toward Mundu. Sahib lifted the phone. Sahib started smashing the cabinet with the phone. Shards of glass rained on the floor. Hundreds of white sugary pills bounced and rolled on the glacial glint of newly shattered objects. Twenty liters of rum and whiskey filled the room, the carpets wicked up 49 homeopathic formulations. "Why did she fucking leave?" General-sahib screamed, slapping Mundu on his cheeks again and again.

"Why?"

Ramji held Mundu by his arm and dragged him to the kitchen.

"Can't take it no more," Mundu showed his reddened cheeks to Ramji.

"Don't go near him when the man is angry."

"I'll go back to my village in Bihar, grow rice or work in a coal mine, at least I'll walk head high," said Mundu.

"Come on, you are young, naïve. Who will marry you if you quit?"

"Who wants to get married ji?"

"Your mother is searching for the girl, no?"

"All she wants is a grandson."

"Simple."

"Difficult."

"Simple. If a woman goes on top of a man, a boy comes out."

"So if a man goes on top of a woman a girl comes out."

"Simple."

"I thought it was the other way."

"First marry then come to me."

"I'm married to the military."

"Bakwaas, nonsense!"

"Why do you stay with him?"

"Stomach."

"No, the real reason?"

"General is not bad. His heart is at right place. He flares up fast, cools down fast. When I was young I too had thin skin like you. Many years ago the Pakistanis had killed five of our boys at the border. The general was a major then—on duty round the clock."

"You mean sahib did some hard work to supplement homeopathy!"

"You have not seen war yet, Mundu; army becomes morose

during peace time. Anyways, those days I used to deliver lunch at his office. One day while I was laying the table a tall private walked in without permission. 'How dare you,' yelled the general..."

"How like him."

"Listen. I'm not finished yet. So the general yelled—where was I? Yes, I felt bad for the private. His khaki uniform was threadbare, faded; the chevron on his shoulder needed a bottle of brasso. Next, I see he walks thirty-nine steps all the way to the Sahib and raises his hands to his face and starts crying. He was shitting in his pants. 'Telegram arrived, sir,' the private sobbed. 'My wife, sir, she gave birth to daughter, sir.' He burst out wailing. A grown up man burst out wailing. 'Sir, the daughter, sir. Dead sir.' Never have I seen a grown up man wail like that. I was really afraid because I thought the general would lock the private in the Quarter Guard and make the private wash his shitty pants. But, sahib did something admirable. He sprung up from his swivel chair and walked towards the private and offered him hope. He held his hand tenderly. When the private calmed down, General-sahib sighed and said: *The world was made in bad taste*."

The lights in the valley had dimmed; only the POW building lights were sodium yellow and bright. The distance between the house and the barracks seemed to have grown. On the veranda the record player needle was scratching against the LP label. Half-dead fireflies swirled inside the half-empty whiskey glass. The general had passed out, his legs crossed on the walnut stool, hands covered with trails of congealed blood. He was snoring rhythmically like the snare drums and bagpipes in the regiment band. Tiny bits of peanuts stuck to his henna-colored handlebar moustache. He looked like a little rat. Together Mundu and Ramji carried him to his bed. Then they returned and cleaned the veranda and the living room with a mop.

Back in the tent they removed their brown canvas shoes, their itchy military socks that smelt of camphor floating in urine. Ramji poured some Johnny Walker in an empty tea cup. He had stolen the whiskey a few days earlier from General-sahib's cabinet.

"Not for me," said Mundu, revolving his little gecko eyes.

"Not for you!"

"Give me the bottle."

"Bot—"

Mundu walked out in darkness on wet grass to the granite rock on the slopes of mountain and sat down and drank the whiskey. He examined the stars above him and began crying. Harder and louder until the bottle rolled away after spilling its contents on his knees. Then he heard the red phone, ringing inside the house.

"General Manto's residence," answered the orderly, standing in the middle of the ruined and flooded room.

"Radio Operator Nair speaking."

"Speak louder, frequency five."

"Listening?"

"Good!"

"Tiger arrived?"

"He arrived at twenty-two hundred hours. Jeep No.1 broke down—"

Tiger's wife ran away with an artisht. Tiger drank whiskey. Tiger demolished his favourite things. Tiger sleeping. Tiger snoring.

Mundu will sleep at zero three hundred hours, wake up at zero six hundred hours. Mundu lives in the fucking world. The world was designed in bad taste.

Mundu sat on sahib's chair on the veranda and turned on his master's favourite record. He crossed his legs on the walnut stool in front of his chair and chewed the leftover peanuts.

Black is black
I want my baby back...
Bad is bad,
That I feel so sad.
It's time, it's time
That I found peace of mind, oh oh
What can I do.
'Cause I'm feeling blue

Still wet from the spilled whiskey, he shivered. The chill had entered his bones. He stumbled into the tent to wipe himself. *Gitmit music. Gitmit musik. Gitmit musak.* He forgot to wipe himself. Instead, he recovered the wet playing cards from his tea mug. He wiped the curdled sugary mess off the cards. He polished them the way he polished sahib's black boots, and then he placed them outside on the slope of the parrot-green tent canvas. The cold wind from the valley was howling mildly, getting stronger. Soon it blew away the drying cards, scattering them on the poppies in the garden.

Watching the cards disappear, Mundu's eyes welled up. "All because of that fucker Manto," he muttered. He walked back to the house, this time with the intention to strangulate Manto. He opened the bedroom door slowly and noiselessly and walked to the head on the bed.

The General was uttering words in his sleep. *Mundu, sorry. Ramji. When she returns, Mundu, all well.*

Mundu listened carefully. He bent over the sleeping general and listened carefully and clearly. He felt a strong urge to do something unprecedented. He bent lower and lower and lower until his lips touched something.

The general muttered: *Mundu. She comes. There.*

Mundu saluted his sahib softly so as not to wake him up, and headed toward the tent. Was it the left cheek? Right? He couldn't tell.

Outside, the wind grew stronger and stronger and within three hours it fled Kashmir towards the ugly Plains, flushing away the darkness and all its stars.

~

Arjun

Arjun raises his hands and feels his turban. He lifts the navy-blue muslin turban by about half an inch, allows his head to breathe. The thing slips back. He rotates it to cover his ears and the nape of his neck and the line that deepens his forehead.

Why can't I do things to my own body? He is talking to himself.

A perturbed crowd surrounds him, pushing and jostling, not an inch of empty space. *Indian Railways.* He notices the bathroom has no door; there is an odor of urine hanging in the train. A miniature fan swivels on the ceiling, rhymes with the clatter of the wheels, hurls hot air on him.

It's my body. Yet Aunty and Grandpa don't want me to take off my turban and cut my hair short. But this time I am ready.

Black smoke loops in now and then, nudges him to lower the window. Aunty G, Grandpa, and Arjun have been in the train for eleven hours already. And now evening invades the villages passing by. Sometimes wind intrudes noisily. Worst is Grandpa's congested breathing, his fits of coughing.

Let them oppose, Aunty and Grandpa don't know the first thing about pain. All they care about is the pain I'll cause them. For them, religion is more important than my body.

Grandpa listens to the news by the hour. Grandpa's sole contribution to society is this listening he does. Even in the train he's glued to news. Stains of mustard cover the brown skin of his transistor; the dial is set on BBC. "These Gohrey-British looted India but their news is honest," the old man keeps muttering.

Impossible to talk to them scientifically. They stop listening after their grand pronouncement, "Sikh boys must never clip their hair; remember, the turban is our identity." They stop listening when I say the turban hurts my ears, turns them red. Every morning a new migraine begins the moment I tie my long hair in a tight knot and stand in front of a mirror and spiral five yards of muslin around my heavy head.

The BBC World Service broadcast phases in and out of the train. Mingling, sometimes with other stations, sometimes with alien tongues. Sometimes the sound is a little faster, or comes to a complete stop before beginning again.

A wheezing reed he's become. Grandpa's lived his life, a fine life. But he must die, die soon to end suffering. He doesn't suffer alone, I too suffer when I see him suffer.

Scalloped in her seat, Aunty G reads a glossy magazine in Punjabi. She keeps reminding Grandpa to redo his turban. His turban is disheveled, but in the faint light glows like a cluster of fireflies

Aunty turns magazine pages noisily, reads noisily, talks noisily. So taken by herself and her ideas is she that she doesn't notice the distress she causes in those around her. Makes people sulk, they withdraw, protest silently.

A passenger, sitting on the floor, puts his paw on the tip of Arjun's foot, which he lifts and shakes. He hates crowds, human thickets. Crowds force perfectly sane people to behave like rabid dogs. He hates Aunty G too when she fusses about him, steps into his space.

He loves Aunty G, but sometimes she makes it impossible for him to focus on chemistry studies at college. His friends don't have problems with their families. His friends have proper parents. He envies them.

The moment we arrive I'll rush to the hairdresser's. My first hair cut. I'll tell her to burn my turban along with my hair. Forget the ashes. When has religion resided in the folds of a turban?

Under Aunty G's eyes he doesn't know just what he is. Perhaps just a bundle of shame. Shame is written all over him. He is ashamed of his body, his turban; his turban an anomaly, an aberration, a discomfort, a migraine. How can one's guardians own one's body, really?

Rekha is right, there is no place to kiss me, not an inch on my face without hair. True, my beard is soft and sparse, but it is a bit dense for the beard of a fourteen-year-old. Strange she loves me despite it.

They met the day monsoons arrived and scrubbed the summer's dust off the trees. For him Rekha is a poem written with cinnamon. Black wavy hair of a coastal girl, narrow eyes, fearless eyebrows. There is a mole on her forehead. She was born with a built-in bindi, he jokes.

"Rekha is a spoiled woman," says Aunty G. "Not even a Sikh."

Grandpa raises the volume of his transistor.

The whole crowd listens to the news:

"India sends first Indian to space."

The whole crowd applauds spontaneously.

"They did it! They did it! Eleven point two kilometres per second...speed at which an object escapes Gravity.

The compartment shakes as the train picks up speed, no, velocity to be precise, because they are headed in a certain direction. A ticket collector appears in the aisle, and like all corrupt civilians, he demands extra money for himself.

"Shame on you," says Grandpa, "my son died for this country."

Embarrassed, the man fakes a fall at Grandpa's feet, turns,

and clears off. Grandpa squeezes his head out of the window and spits.

The ticket collector resembles Uncle G. Uncle is an aeronautical engineer. He escaped to Milwaukee, America. Tall, pot-bellied, gel on hair. A Cut-Surd, clean-shaven. Arjun has seen him smiling by the Houdini museum. As soon as the photo arrived in mail, Aunty G destroyed it, tore it to pieces. She erases whatever doesn't suit her.

To the world she still displays Uncle G in a turban, a much younger version, the time when tufts of fresh beard had barely touched his face, a baby face.

"Uncle looks smarter in his turban," says Aunty G.

"He will re-turban himself when he returns back from wretched West."

Aunty G never informed Grandpa when Uncle G crossed the turban line. To prevent that fatal attack of asthma.

Arjun could escape to America too, like Uncle G; but he is petrified by the idea. Grandpa is old; his beard, like his hair, is becoming brittle, his hands are almost sponge-like. And Aunty G, she is growing old too. The capillaries on her arms have turned purple-blue. Underneath the coat of henna, her hair is gray.

His Aunty and Grandpa no longer talk about Mother and Father. Their approach to pain is to pretend there is none until it becomes blurred or so indistinct that new pain swallows the old.

It didn't pain Arjun the day his parents were killed by a land-mine at the border. But every day the pain grows, ever since he read about landmines in *Irreversible Thermodynamics*. He barely recalls Father's build, but the face and voice are still with him. Mother, too.

PFM-1, made in Soviet Union, the pressure-sensitive blast mine, looks like a toy, almost a butterfly. Father and Mother stepped on the veiled butterfly. A lightning flash. Shower of mud, vaporized tissue, burnt flesh.

Father was brave and stylish in everything he did, even with his turban. He tied his turban like the Maharajah of Patiala. And he took care of Aunty G, Grandpa, Mother, and Arjun. Now Arjun must take care. Just one more year before he graduates from junior college. One more year before he begins the honors degree in chemistry.

"A turban is our passport," Father used to say. "Passport is a book. One must never destroy a book."

Arjun turns towards Grandpa. BBC news announces fire in a British stadium during a cricket match between India and Pakistan.

No way!... How did the flames spread in the stadium? Rapidly? Slowly? What were the conditions of combustion? What led to H_2O+CO_2? Is that all? Things burn, stop burning, flames shoot upwards, smoke rises. What would flames look like in the absence of gravity?

The train arrives at Panipat station. Portraits of Mrs. Indira Gandhi and other Congress leaders dirty the walls of the station. He peers out of the window and buys a glass of tea from the one-eyed vendor. Mrs. Gandhi attacked the Golden Temple, she damaged the most sacred space of the Sikhs.

Whenever Aunty G sees Mrs. G's photo in a paper, she tears out the entire face. She ignores Arjun's protests, his call to reason.

"Why," she asks, "for the crimes of one-two Sikhs has the widow Prime Minister labeled the entire Sikh community terrorists?"

Not true, Aunty, Mrs G's bodyguards are Sikhs.

A pack of paper boys appears on the platform, yelling scams and scandals. The train shows no sign of movement. Indian

Railways. Yesterday's trains arriving today. His eyes simmer and expand in the heat, then tumble lazily towards the crowd outside.

There is a strange woman on the platform. Short, thin, speckles on her skin. She's wearing a wrinkled salwar-kameez, no dupatta. Is surprisingly clean, no flies or mosquitoes swarming around her. A platform woman, one of those platformers who hang around the railway terminals not for begging or thieving, but because deep down they are unable to conceive of the notion of home.

Suddenly the strange woman starts flattening dough with a rolling pin. Sprays some flour and flattens it further. There is no flour or dough around her, yet she pretends everything is there, in its proper place. After flattening the flour she picks up an imaginary broken glass bangle or a knife or a pebble from the platform and starts sharpening it.

I too will turn mad, mad, mad ... if I fail this time, fail to act.

The train surges forward. Views of buttes and mesas vanish abruptly. Views of muddy ink-colored ponds and semi-naked children swish by like leonid showers.

Perhaps Rekha won't like me without long hair. We've talked about it. But Rekha can be capricious at times.

Last time, she teased him. "Go become a Buddhist monk. Tonsure-headed, claret-robed, calm-faced Tibetan monk."

The crowd around him gets noisier. How can one afford to chat endlessly in this world? The one sane person in the train is the blind soot-daubed beggarman singing in the aisle for money. The aisle has become a wave of people sitting on suitcases. Rows ahead of him an old peasant rubs his cataract eyes. *So that is where it all ends...* Fear swirls around him, twitches his forehead, rubs his turban. He calculates the probability of his success.

A little girl distracts him. She occasionally peers inside the compartment and hides behind the door.

"What's your name?"

"Naseem."

"Where are you coming from?"

"Kashmir."

"Where are you going?"

"Delhi."

"What are you doing?"

"Playing."

"No, no, what are you doing with that maroon cloth?"

"Tying a turban on my doll, like yours."

He is sick agonizing over a yard of cloth. And he still doesn't know how he'll show Aunty G his new face. Probably Uncle G never returns from America because he can't look Aunty and Grandpa in the eye.

"Stop," shouts Grandpa, "listen, listen to this." The train slackens a bit, then starts rolling silently as if on Teflon tracks.

BBC NEWS: *"Indian Prime Minister Mrs. Indira Gandhi is dead. She was assassinated early this morning by her Sikh bodyguards. There are reports that Mrs. Gandhi's party members are retaliating against the Sikh community throughout India."*

They enter the carriage spitting like maharajahs, they spit on Sikh berths, urinate on Sikh baggage.

"You bloody traitors, you killed our Mother, we'll revenge blood with blood."

The old peasant with cataract eyes, not a Sikh, battles against the mob.

"Tomorrow we've to live with these people, don't you know, you fools, tomorrow, who do you plan to live with?"

They kick him aside, identify all Sikhs in the carriage, order non-Sikhs out on the platform. Then they tie Sikh hands to iron rods with ropes, play soccer with turbans, and start shaving their heads.

Heads of Aunty G, Grandpa, Arjun. Heads: of autodriver's wife, schoolteacher's son, wheat farmer's father, soldier's daughter. Heads that scream but give up all resistance after the first strand of hair is cut. After the first strand, heads that almost help the surgeons operating on them. Locks of hair pile up, whirl around, the world feels lighter.

Arjun frees his hands, hides in between bundles and suitcases, invisible to the mob.

The Congress-wallah leading the thugs orders his fellows to step out of the train. Then he douses kerosene on the screaming bodies.

"This will teach you killers a lesson," he shouts. His Gandhi-Nehru khadi flutters while he rips pages from Aunty G's magazine, strikes a match, sets the pages on fire, lets them loose. He steps out himself, then locks the carriage.

Flames and smoke dart through the carriage, ignite known and unknown things, men, women, children. Flames, now against gravity, hop-scotching; now striking like lightning; now engulfing Grandpa's transistor.

But Grandpa's transistor refuses to shut up. Its dial continues to dance, steps in and out of the BBC, then stomps over to All India Radio.

All India Radio announces the assassination followed by classical music and *"Situation in country continues to be calm and peaceful. Barring a few chut-phut small incidents no retaliation has been reported against the Sikh community."*

Arjun gives up his search for Aunty G and Grandpa. There are cylinders of fire all around him. He has never seen all differences between people vanish so fast. He hears his name burning on someone's lips, hurries towards her with a sheet, but it is too late. She flames up before him from head to toe, one last time, then ceases.

Grandpa rises from a pile of bodies, beckons Arjun with his charred hand.

"Escape before it is too late. You can do it through the hole, the toilet hole," he whispers before his lungs collapse, inwards.

Arjun crawls through bodies and molten plastic towards the bathroom; scoops up a handful of hair and throws it. He then kicks several burning turbans up in the air. The turbans fall not as turbans, but as leonids from outer space.

Really? Fascinating. No. The leonids, depending on velocity, reach a temperature of 10,000°C. They survive intense scorching because they pass heat to air. This makes air molecules fluoresce. But air is a bad conductor, can not conduct heat away fast enough. Most heat remains on surface, therefore, the leonids melt, vaporize...

Lifetime of leonids = 3 sec

Visible as glowing leonids = 1/10 sec

Arjun, while watching leonids, weeps, refuses to make a wish. He is listening to the dead and dying. He is listening to the ugly unconscious of his country unfolding. He worms his way towards the wide Indian-style toilet. The hole, coated with molecules of urine, shit, and ammonia, spits him out on the tracks. His body hurts on sharp stones. Grandpa's transistor is his sole possession on the tracks. The platform woman has observed his fall. Her head is loaded with bundles of muslin, imaginary bundles. She smashes the bundles on the rocks and rushes towards him and runs her fingers on the lines of fear on his face. She readjusts his turban. There is no turban, yet she pretends there is an unnaturally large creature on his head. It will take a year for his hair to grow back, she tells him.

~

Small Pain

Lady Doctor Nooria Gul Naz was dressed in her luminous nightgown, eating dried fruit, when General Manto's chauffeur knocked on her door.

"It is past midnight. But wait. I need five minutes," she told the man and rushed to her bedroom. She dressed exactly the way she dressed for the army hospital in the mornings. Plain uniform sari, khaki-colored, with silver epaulettes on the blouse. She rolled her hair in a bun and hid it neatly under the brown cap. Ever since she joined the army she had stopped beautifying herself. She was a short woman, four feet eleven, and on that night she looked shorter than usual despite walking in two-inch heels to the jeep parked outside her house.

The general's mother, wrapped in a black shawl, was sitting on the front seat. She looked over her shoulder and waved at the Lady Doctor. Gul Naz surrendered her medical bag to the chauffeur. The man opened the rear door and helped her settle down on the immaculate leather seat. Then he drove like a bird to the general's residence, which stood on the slope of Sulphur Mountain.

"Don't worry," the old woman reassured the Lady Doctor on the way, "I'll be in the same room when you examine him."

The last time Gul Naz examined a man was during her residency days at the Medical College in Srinagar, the summer capital of the province. At the army hospital all her patients were women, morbid regiment wives, who only visited during the day.

"Is it serious?" Gul Naz asked, rubbing her eyes.

"You will find out," said the old woman.

A sentry opened the tall metal gate and guided the jeep in. The beams lit up the enormous yellow stucco mansion and the figure of the orderly, standing on the veranda. The orderly rushed toward the two women and clicked his heels before Gul Naz, whose rank was that of a captain. He then helped the formidable old woman out of the jeep.

"Take Doctor-sahiba to the drawing room," the old woman instructed. "Serve her strong coffee to wake her up. Meanwhile I will prepare your sahib. Wait. Where are you going? Carry Doctor-sahiba's medical bag."

"No. No," said the Lady Doctor.

Inside, the air was stagnant, dead like the trophies of a hunter. Stag antlers on the wall startled Gul Naz as she paced the drawing room, her heels clicking. She opened the window. A cold breeze stirred the curtains, which entangled her elbows.

"I should have picked up General Manto's medical file from the hospital," she reprimanded herself.

The lights shimmering in the valley below left her with a mild vertigo. She recoiled, sat on the sofa, suffused by pale light. On her left side stood a large and dark painting, propped against a chair. She examined the woman in the painting. The woman had a narrow face with stern features and a slightly crooked nose. In her left hand were three perfectly red fruits. The eyes of the woman gazed down as if they had just seen a naked man. Gul Naz leaned closer. Behind the woman the artist had applied enormous paint on the trees, which resembled trapezoids, vertical coffins more or less. Limbs of people jutted out of the cracks in the trapezoids. Gul Naz had heard through rumors in the regiment that the painting was done by the general's ex-wife.

"Madam," said the orderly, "coffee is served." He left an oval tray, with a silver gleam, on the center table. As she stirred sugar she noticed the bare space on the wall where the painting once hung.

The coffee stung her palate like barbed wire. She closed her eyes. She felt she was becoming a part of the painting. The orderly's urgent voice broke her concentration, "Madam, General-sahib is ready."

"Five minutes," she said. She consumed the fluid a bit too quickly, burning the tip of her tongue. She wiped her lips with a starched napkin and placed the cup upside down on the tray. Then she closed her eyes again and said a silent prayer to Allah.

She had joined the army hospital because it was the only institution in the region that did not create a fuss about degrees from unrecognized medical colleges. In the beginning she had enjoyed her job, but as of late, she had come to hate it. The officers' wives had started asking her too many questions about her divorce. Six regiment men had sent marriage proposals to the hospital through the wives of fellow officers. She could not muster the courage to resign. Resigning was not a real option. "Prepare for a *total* war with Pakistan," the general had announced in the regiment. What kept her going were her morbid patients and their confessions.

"Madam," interrupted the orderly, "Sahib says his pain is growing."

She arose from the sofa, adjusted the pleats of her sari and followed the orderly's boots. The man was at least a head taller than she was. He swung open the bedroom door, and there behind the old woman was the general, half-reclining on his bed. A floral-patterned blanket covered his legs. He was drinking scotch to ease his pain. Certainly not winning the battle.

Gul Naz saluted.

The general drained his glass and closed one eye, the way hunters do while taking aim.

"Sit down, Lady Doctor," he said. "We bothered you because all the men doctors are away to the front."

"You better tell her the truth," said the old woman rocking her chair.

Gul Naz's body shrank to encourage the truth but neither the mother nor her son uttered a word. She broke the silence with, "We forgot to pick up your file from the hospital, sir."

"Happens," said the general. "Mundu can bring it up."

She approached the door and issued special instructions to the big-jawed orderly. The man could not hide a murderous expression that spread over his face as he clicked his heels and disappeared downhill.

"Where is the pain, sir?"

"Here," said the general, his palm on his chest.

Gul Naz sat on the sofa. She placed the medical bag on her lap and took out a few gizmos. The general stared at the curves of the stethoscope in her small hands.

Pale light filled the room. On the left side of the general's bed was a glass cabinet overflowing with bottles of rum and scotch. Stuffed birds hugged the wall facing the bed. Beneath the birds was the old woman's rocking chair and next to it was the sofa.

Gul Naz took a few steps to the bed and said with some authority, "Lie down fully, sir."

Her patient obeyed. He slipped down on the bed and looked at the papier-mâché ceiling. He tried to smile as she rolled up his checked kurta. She felt his chest with her hands. She applied cautious pressure on his abdomen, all the way to the string of his pyjama. She listened with the stethoscope to the crackles and murmurs emerging from his heart. She tapped her fingers just below his nipples as if she was playing the tabla. "Bastard," she said to herself, "his glass is never empty and yet his heart is right as rain." Could it be the phantom pain? She was well aware of the phantom phenomenon. Many soldiers developed pains in their chests around the time their yearly cardiology reports were due.

"Girl," interrupted the patient's mother, "the pain is in his foot."

Gul Naz looked bewildered.

"Lift the blanket," said the old woman. "He always hides his pain. This time is no exception. Ever since he was a boy he has hidden his pain."

"There, there, Mother," protested the general, rubbing his chin. "I hid it because our Lady Doctor was trained in an un-recognized medical college, what do you call it, the donation college. I wanted to test her skills. I must say she passed like a tigress."

Gul Naz hid her annoyance beneath a clinical smile as she lifted the blanket and crouched over the left foot.

"How did this happen, sir?"

"Small thing," said the general, pressing his lips, "really small."

Gul Naz sat on the edge of the bed and placed the medical bag on her knees. She pulled out a roll of cotton and a scalpel.

The general surveyed her body curiously. He felt young again. Between him and Gul Naz was less than a foot. A foot, not including her thin sari. He leaned against the pillow and smiled.

"Your ring frightens me, Lady Doctor," he said, grasping her hand firmly.

She shook her locked hand. The scalpel fell on the floor.

"You left your husband, didn't you?"

This was the first time an army officer had crossed the respect-able distance and dared to be so direct about her divorce. Gul Naz glanced over her shoulder at the general's mother, but the old woman kept rocking her chair. The general placed his glass on

Gul Naz's epaulette.

"Madam!" she raised her voice, "see what Sir is doing."

"Lady Doctor," the old woman beckoned her with a finger, "come to me."

The general let her go.

"Open the windows," she said, "let the breeze come in."

Gul Naz did exactly as she was told.

"Sit by me," said the old woman.

Sweat broke on her face as she sat on the sofa.

"This son of mine was very sad today," said the old woman. "It was the anniversary of his separation. So I took him to the Sufi saint's grave where I prayed for the return of his wife. She was a witch, that woman. But this evening I said to hell with it and I prayed because I care for the boy's happiness. When we came back his mood was certainly better. He sat in the drawing room, asked the orderly to pull off his boots and make him a drink. Suddenly, after the second glass, he started looking at her portrait on the wall. He stood under the heavy frame and kept looking—looking until the wretched thing fell on his foot and he screamed. I told you she was a witch."

There was a hesitant knock on the door. The orderly stuck his head into the room.

"Wait," said the general.

Mother stopped rocking her chair and said in a hushed tone, "Don't drink scotch from the bottle."

"Mother, I know how to drink scotch."

"You don't."

"Enter," said the general.

The orderly clicked his heels and said, "Sir, the hospital clerk has arrived to deliver the file, sir."

"Bring him in," instructed the general.

Gul Naz saw a red file in an unsteady hand. The hand belonged to an elderly man, who wore a white laboratory coat and looked as if he had not slept since the occupation of Kashmir.

"Evening, sir."

"Give it to the Lady Doctor," said the general. "That will do. Listen, ask my jeep-wallah to drop you at the hospital. Dis-miss."

"Jai Hind, sir."

The old woman's voice chirped again. She seemed to be in a hurry. It was not easy to understand her as she revealed her false teeth. "I am sending the girl back to examine you," she said. "Behave this time."

Her son shook his head.

"Go now," she turned to Gul Naz, who stirred on the sofa like a creature alone in a remote and desolate area. "He won't harm you. When he was a little boy he wanted to become a juggler. He couldn't even keep his wife."

Gul Naz eyed the woman with panic and wonder. She thrust the file in her bag and inched slowly to the bed. She bent over the general's left foot, picked up the scalpel from the floor and cut open the bandage. She pulled off the blood-stained absorbent that was surprisingly heavy. The trapezoidal shape of the absorbent reminded her of the coffin-like trees in the painting. An eerie feeling stirred inside her. The general tried to make a pleasant face. "Small pain. Really. Not as bad as the pain this crazy place has given me, Lady Doctor," he said. "You know I am a motivated soldier. Everyone knows. But I cannot do my job well in Kashmir because every day it shows me its claws. Lady Doctor, our army requires a better commander, no?"

She threw the absorbent in the bin.

"Lady Doctor, you are a Kashmiri," said the general. "What are the people saying about me?"

"Honestly, sir," she said while examining the wound with a cone of light, "they are not saying nice things."

She felt the wound was a textbook situation. "Sir, even the papers—"

"Do you believe everything you read in the papers?" asked the general.

"Sir, I—"

"Lies," said the old woman.

"Allegations, Mother."

"Lies," said the old woman.

"Madam," hesitated Gul Naz, "last week, fifty-three girls were raped by the jawans in our regiment."

"Lies," said the old woman.

"The press-wallahs are pushing this story," said the general. "They should be hanged."

A dense feeling of unease came over Gul Naz. The cap on her head was not wide enough to contain the intensity of her anger. The general tilted his head and measured her entire body with a nervous glance. She measured his distinguished face with disgust. She did not hear his embarrassed laughter while applying an ointment on the wound. Her hands began rebandaging his foot.

"LIES, girl," said the old woman. "Do you know who you are talking to?"

"Shut up, Mother!" said the general. "The Lady Doctor doesn't mean a word of what she said. We will not court martial her."

"Sorry, sir," she said, her hand on her mouth.

"Lady Doctor, you have guts," said the general. "I like women who have guts. I like you Kashmiris. But, you see this place is going through a major surgery. We are the nursing orderlies. Peace is our profession. The army is here not to eliminate a people because their noses are sharper. Honest advice, whenever in doubt, look at the facts. Actions speak louder than words. You, Lady Doctor, are a living proof of how well we treat the locals."

Gul Naz sat on the sofa and slowly turned on the lamp on the marble table. A circle of bright light swelled around her. She placed the medical bag on her lap and pulled out the red file. Solemnly, she began leafing through the interminable contents. The latest cardiology report was in it. She was surprised the file did not have the general's name on the label. The thing belonged to some other officer, a colonel by rank. A vague image of the sleep-starved clerk flashed through her mind. "Mix-up," she said to herself. A cold breeze stirred the curtains by the window and percolated through her sari. Then something clicked in Gul Naz's mind and she kept looking for a long time in the direction of the painting in the adjacent room. "Allah is not going to like me for what I am going to tell the general," she said to herself. "Let Him not," said the woman in the painting. "Stick to the mix-up. The general deserves it, the bastard."

"Sir," said Gul Naz with a surge of confidence, "X-ray is necessary to determine if the foot joint is damaged."

"I see," said the general.

"But, even if the joint is damaged," she said emphatically, "I won't recommend the operation."

"No?"

"Because—" she stopped in mid-sentence. She covered the wrong name on the file with her thumb, stepped to the edge of the bed, and shared the report with the general. "Because of this. Your heart has enlarged. Cardiomyopathy. The foot operation will require general anesthesia. It might kill you."

"My God. My God," said the old woman clutching her black shawl. She stopped rocking her chair.

"Lady Doctor," said the general with a forced smile, "what I don't understand is why the other doctor never informed me this?"

"Sir."

"Without the operation how long will my foot hurt?"

"Intense pain will last two months only. Then it might become intermittent," she said.

"After X-ray we will know better."

"I see," said the general. A film of tears filled his icy eyes. He looked like a tired and broken man.

"The pain in foot is nothing, sir, it might even strengthen your heart."

She was feeling lighter. She scribbled on a white sheet the names of medicines and ointments and handed it to the orderly. Her handwriting was so bad, she herself had problems deciphering it.

The examination concluded with a silence. The general opened a new scotch and asked the orderly to wrap the painting in the drawing room and hand it to the chauffeur for delivery at the doctor's residence.

"In army," he said, "this is the only way to say thank you."

"But, sir," she said, "the portrait belongs to your wife."

"Ex-wife."

Gul Naz picked up her bag, and felt the weight of guilt. She averted her gaze as she took leave of the general.

"Minor pain," he said, raising his glass.

"Jai Hind!"

The old woman walked with the Lady Doctor to the jeep. "You are a nice girl," she said. "You should get married. We don't believe in dowry. The only thing we demand is that you change your religion."

Gul Naz gasped and settled comfortably on the front seat. "He doesn't have long to live," she whispered in the old woman's ear through the side window. The chauffeur turned on the ignition. "According to the report, not more than a year," she said pitilessly. "Please do not tell him. Do not talk to him. No one should be allowed to talk to him. He needs silence. He needs—"

The three-headed lion on Gul Naz's cap bounced up and down along with her body as the jeep stopped on the cobbled path in front of her residence. The chauffeur leapt to his feet to assist her. Inside, she unwrapped the painting and placed it on her bed. The varnished wooden frame was splitting apart, but the canvas was so clean, it gleamed like a mirror and she could see her trembling face in it. She thought about the bare space on the general's wall where the painting once hung and examined the growing dread within her, which had vanished only for a while during that sweet moment of revenge.

~

Parachute Aunty

Her daughter, Maya, is pregnant again.

The old woman slowly opens the jasmine-scented curtains. She surveys the dust-coated amaltass trees outside the miserable hospital. *Crazy trees,* she mutters. *Not a single leaf stirring, despite the wind. Just like Maya.*

She walks back to her daughter's bed. She wants to mutter something to her sleeping child, but the wind has silenced her. She has yet to tell Maya that when her own belly was pregnant, she didn't want the baby.

"Is my daughter out of danger?" the old woman asks.

"Yes, Aunty!" says the nurse.

Only yesterday, Maya was returning home from the bazaar —with fruits in bags and baby in the belly—when men in a speeding jeep honked and stared and whistled. Maya lost her balance and fell. The fruits slowly rolled away from her, clogging the street. Maya lifted the hem of her sari. Thick, dark blood covered her knees. She placed both hands on her belly and wept.

"No Aunty, not all blood squeezing out means *miscarriage,*" the nurse reassures her. "Look Aunty, Maya's sonographs are flickering nicely."

"When will she open eyes?"

The old woman sits by the bed and buries her only ear in

Maya's belly. She hears wind howling in a tunnel. Sound of butterfly wings. A downpour of lizards, of tiny swans. The old woman's body expands, almost explodes into dance. But her feet can't fly any more; her legs, too, suffer from palsy. Roots run between the bottom of her feet and the ground beneath the hospital.

"Are you closely attached to your daughter?" asks the nurse.

"Meaning?"

"Have you read each other's diaries?"

"What use are the diaries if someone else ends up reading them?"

She decides to put the story in a letter.

Listen Maya, time has come for me to tell you a story. Promise me you will wake up to read it. I won't stop writing until you wake up...

Once upon a time, your mother, when she was a general's wife, used to climb a hill in Kashmir. Normally officers' wives play pupplu, rummy, and other card games, but, I, General Manto's wife, would climb the hill. I would walk past the barbed wire military camp, past the Sufi saint's grave, all the way to the ruins of the ancient monastery. I would climb the ruins barefooted, with shoes in my hands. The walls were so weak, red-rocks dislodged and ants fell to the ground as I climbed. At the highest point, I would stand calm and still; my sari rustled in the wind.

Then I would jump.

"Parachute Aunty! Parachute Aunty," the village children would cheer me on.

My sari puffed up on the way down.

Jumping became a ritual. Every morning, the village children, who lived just a furlong away from the barracks, when they saw me climb, pulled back their kites and gathered to watch the spectacle.

I loved watching them watch me; I loved the runny noses of half-naked village children.

The Sufi saint's grave was perhaps a dog's grave. Over the period of time a single truth and many lies twisted into a single lie and many truths—and as a result, the villagers started worshipping the grave.

I am sorry, Maya, at that time I sought to be free of the pit of worms within me, bury it next to the saint, have it worshipped. That's why I jumped.

The creature living inside me was so alien and unnatural and I knew no trick to expel it. Overnight, my body had swollen into one of those fat Buddhas sold in Ladakh. Externally, I was swelling, but internally I felt as if I was splitting. No, I wasn't ready yet for splitting into smaller and smaller things, first into two, then four, then eight.

Your father was an HMV, *as the modern generation says—His Mother's Voice. Mother-in-law followed us like a shadow. Mother-in-law was with us on our honeymoon.*

My first night with him: I woke in the dark. Mother-in-law, with her mouth half-open, was sandwiched between me and the son.

"This is not your bed," I tapped on mother-in-law's shoulder.

Mother-in-law opened her mouth wider and turned towards her son and drew up her knees to her chest.

"Aren't you ashamed?" I asked.

Mother-in-law heard nothing, kept chattering her teeth. Me, I spread two quilts over them and wept.

Maya, some mornings I desired the creature inside me; it felt precious, I didn't want to damage it. I extended my stop-overs on top of the ruins before the jump. My delays and indecisions made the children impatient. I could have shooed them away with a fistful of Parlé toffees. I didn't. I loved to hear this applause; it gave me the impetus to jump. In school and college I used to dance for applause.

"Kathak-kali," your father would call me before marriage.

"Change your name," mother-in-law made him say.

"Don't smell the yellow roses," mother-in-law made him say.

"Women your age don't dance," mother-in-law made him say.

"Touch my mother's feet and ask for blessings," mother-in-law made him say. I never touched the swollen, eczema-crusted feet. For a while I found diversion in painting, as I had as a child. As happened then, my wounds became colors on the canvas. But at the end of the day, painting did not turn out to be a real diversion. I saw you crawling on the canvases, repeating my life.

Sometimes I would sit on the veranda for long hours and listen to the road down in the valley. At night I would watch Bombay films. The open-air theatre was visible from the veranda.

It was then I decided to fall in love. I asked the orderly to smuggle into our house hundreds of film posters from the projectionist's room. I filled the bedroom with big stars. You might recognize some names— Dilip Kumar, Guru Dutt, Dharmendra, Rajesh Khanna, Sunil Dutt, Shashi Kapoor, Dev Anand, Sanjeev Kumar, Rajnikanth.

"It is not a decent thing to do," mother-in-law made him say.

"Why are there no actresses?" mother-in-law made him say.

Rather than ripping off the posters I continued acquiring more and more of them. I asked the orderly to fill the bathroom with all the popular villains in the movies. I was falling in love with the villains too. Shatrughan Sinha, Danny, Ranjit, Pran, Gabbar Singh.

"Have you lost your mind?" mother-in-law made him say.

"The actors watch you taking your baths," mother-in-law made him say.

The more they resisted, the mother and son, the more I demonstrated my love. I filled the kitchen with topless men. Slowly the posters started spilling into the veranda. Even the comedians I did not leave behind. Johnny Walker, Asrani, Jagdeep, I.S. Johar.

One day after my bath I confronted my mother-in-law with the truth.

"The baby doesn't belong to your son," I said. "It belongs to one of the stars."

"Get out, go away," mother-in-law made him say.

"Yes," I cried, "I must find the father of my child."

One day, Maya, not knowing what else to do, I left them. I didn't even announce my intention to leave. Why? Perhaps for your sake. Perhaps for you I sacrificed my whole life. Why? Why do you hate me so much. Why?.... Oh, let me not, my dear, leap ahead of my story. Our story.

Baytee, I should have consulted the military gynaecologist; the Lady Doctor might have understood the need for abortion. Instead, one night while mother-in-law and her son were asleep, I decided to end two lives. I stepped out with a lantern. I raised the wick to the size of cinnamon. To this day the smell of kerosene in the lantern flares in my nostrils. That smell accompanied me to the monastery ruins. Together we attempted to expel the stranger from my womb.

Baytee, I raised the lantern, climbed the ruins; I could have climbed blindfolded but that night my body was not strong enough to reach the top. Voices of the village children hit me as if they were little foxes, howling: Parachute Aunty, Parachute Aunty. Eject. Be expelled.

I touched my belly. One, two, three, four...

I jumped.

Upside-down. My head led my body; I inverted the parachute.

Downside-up: The little-dancer, Maya, you inside me.

Airborne for a fraction of a second —almost gliding— we knitted the night to the things on which it fell, we knitted the red rocks together, rebuilt the waters.

Your mother's legs came together and parted.

Then into the sea we toppled, a wave of sharp pain arose, broke, receded. O, what have I done, I said. I lifted the hem of my sari. Thick blood covered my knees. Dark spots enveloped my eyes.

I placed both hands on my belly and wept.

—Baby, I cried.

The voice inside me went still.

—*Baby, do you listen?*

My hands had collided with the earth before my knees did. I crawled on patches of torn kites, grass, pebbles, gasping, then dropped down in prone posture of a yogin practicing shav-asana. The chill of the earth entered my mushy bones.

Un..ka..

I heard a cry.

Ka..fa..ka.. Shhhh...

I felt a merciless kick.

—*Baby, yes. Baby, speak, my most determined baby in the world, speak. I am not me; I am you. I exist only for you.*

Maya, it was then you stirred softly and you were vocal again and said something.

Something about the day you would show your tongue to Ma, Ma, MaMa, and make me fall in love despite everything.

But, baytee, our love is the love that blooms only when bodies begin to fail or fall. Where would we be without wounds, diseases, swellings?

She dozed off over the letter.

~

Remover of Obstacles

Last August Mrs. Chintamani was dusting the marble idol of Lord Ganesha in her apartment, when thoughts of obtaining a new husband crossed her mind. She was a young widow, only twenty-nine years old. She lived in a small factory town in the foothills of the Himalayas. The residential colony was established by RATH Agri-Toxics and Chemicals Ltd, a pesticide giant. Locals called it the pesticide colony.

Mrs. Chintamani brought to mind all the suitable bachelors in the colony. She lit camphor and vowed to fast every Tuesday and Friday if she found a charming man. A new husband was a small thing to ask from the generous god. Some years ago, a more audacious widow, Mrs. Indira Priyadarshini Gandhi, had asked for the prime ministership of the country and had received it from the elephant-headed god, the god with cosmic memory, the one who swallows the sorrows of the world, the god with thirty-two names, the remover of obstacles.

Mrs. Chintamani had inherited the Ganesha idol from her great-grandmother. It was the size of a newborn baby. She kept it elevated on the living room mantle. She was more attached to the idol than to her husband, who had worked as a foreman at the pesticide factory until his untimely death. He had left behind a bank balance of eleven rupees, having drunk his wife's dowry money when he was alive through more than two thousand liters of Johnny Walker. Worse, he didn't leave a single child behind. She yearned for a baby to rebuild the ruins of her life.

After six months of mourning, she reclaimed her slender and beautiful body. The aura of the crematorium no longer enveloped her. She emitted the fragrance of earth that arrives with the monsoons. Coconut oil, rubbed on the curls of her hair, glistened. The fingernail marks on her breasts left behind by the dead foreman faded to a memory. That night, August 15, Mrs. Chintamani allowed herself the finest brassiere in the wardrobe and forgot to remove it before sinking into the bed.

She was not alone in the apartment. Her female cousin, Vidya, who had come to live with her after Chintamani's death, was lying on the cheap Kashmiri rug in the living room. She liked Vidya's caring attitude, naughty playfulness, and honesty, but she found it hard to confide in her. Vidya couldn't keep anything in her belly.

At midnight, Mrs. Chintamani dreamt she saw Ganesha meandering through the pesticide colony. Ganesha looked hungry, craving milk. She determined a way to offer him milk. She awoke and slid out of the bed and glided to the living room. She stood before the marble idol for a long time. She unhooked her bra. She cupped her heaving milk-white breasts. She examined the wide aureoles, cinnamon-colored and puckered.

The idol compelled her to lift it in her arms. She yielded. She rocked the baby. She heard the baby's breathing getting harder and harder. She listened to the suckling sounds. Her nipple wiggled in the mouth of cold marble.

"From now on, you all must feed me milk—from breasts, from bowls, from spoons," said the idol. She had no doubt she heard the idol. She was at once astonished and afraid.

Vidya witnessed the incident with wide-open eyes. She wanted to announce the miracle from the balcony. But the widow went down on her knees and begged her cousin not to reveal the news to the colony-wallahs. "Even if I don't tell," said Vidya, "Ganesha himself will tell the people."

Next day the milk started to vanish. Mrs. Chintamani maintained that whenever she left milk in a bowl next to Ganesha, not a single drop remained. At first, she suspected Vidya. Naughtiness has its limits, she told the culprit bluntly. But milk continued to vanish even after locking her cousin in the barn for two nights. This made fear crawl into her face. She closed the windows and stayed indoors.

But soon she ran out of milk and vegetables. That is the only reason she stepped out on the street. Her starched sari flapped in the warm afternoon breeze as she walked toward the bazaar. She heard the colony-wallahs talking in hushed tones. Doors and windows opened one by one. Men, women, and children leaned out of balconies to watch her. She was terrified. Even in the bazaar people behaved strangely. She bought milk, vegetables, basil, fennel, flakes of chilli, but the vendors refused to charge her a single paisa.

On the way back, she rested for a while under the shade of bougainvilleas. She wiped her face with the pallu of her sari. She contemplated the night of the miracle. When she opened her eyes she found herself flocked by children. It was then she thought of consulting the Saffron Politico, the local chief of the civil police, who enforced the customs sanctioned by the conservatives in the community.

The Politico ran his affairs from a large air-conditioned tent, pitched in the empty plot next to the residential area. The tent interior was littered with photographs of saints, scholars and scoundrels. Hung on the canvas were twenty-six ancient swastikas. He wore saffron-colored robes. Vermillion dots and five parallel lines of ash crowded his forehead. On seeing her enter, he clamped himself tight in the lotus posture.

"Strange things are happening," she said after greeting him with folded hands.

"Madam, tell us everything," he said raising his hand to his mouth.

"Milk is disappearing from my apartment every night. Could it be the ghosts?"

The Politico stared at the widow with amusement.

"Ghosts don't drink milk, madam," he clarified. "It is Lord Ganesha himself."

"Answer me seriously," she demanded.

"Miracle, madam. Same is happening here. Same in Dubai. Same in U.S."

"Enough," she said realigning the pallu of her incongruous white sari.

"Shed all false humility, madam. The miracle was set in motion by yourself only." Every word he uttered exuded the authority of a pundit.

"So?" she said. Her breath quickened.

"You don't seem to know what the whole colony knows. Vidya told us everything. Lactation of Lord Ganesha. Forgotten already?"

Her lips quivered. She overreacted the way timid people do when they lose patience in public. "No decent man talks this way. Have you no shame?"

"Enough, madam; here, read *The Times* paper."

The 'phenomenon' initiated by Mrs. Chintamani, the young widow, in the small Himalayan town continues to happen even in New York. An Indian-American reporter drove to the temple in Jackson Heights and witnessed a virtual stampede. When he offered milk to Lord Ganesha in a stainless steel spoon, it was sucked up like someone was drinking it with a straw.

Printed words convinced her of the miracle. She returned to the pesticide colony thanking Ganesha that he had chosen her as a vehicle for his compassion. In her mind she pardoned Vidya for spreading the word. Close to the stairway, she met her eccentric neighbor, Arjun Singh.

"Namasté," he said. His polished black shoes had filaments of pesticide on them; his turban was deep blue.

She returned his greeting with a smile.

"Let me carry the vegetable bag, Madam," he extended his hand. She refused his generous offer with a nod. Then by way of starting a small conversation, she said, "Arjun ji, vegetables taste like poison these days."

"Madam," he asked as they climbed the stairs, "do you wash them before cooking?"

"With gallons of water," she replied looking straight into his face.

"Not all pesticides are water-soluble," he said. "Wash your spinach with oil."

"And how do I wash away oil?"

"Easy," he said. "Allow me to demonstrate."

"Arjun ji, how will oil remove the pesticide in MILK?"

"A trace is a small price to pay for progress."

"Arjun ji, pesticides are deadly; Lord Ganesha has returned to this world to make it pure again."

"Madam," he clarified, "idols are made of marble only."

"Namasté," she said shutting the door behind her.

"We should talk more," he said.

"Less talk, the better."

For Arjun Singh the Ganesha idol was merely a cold inanimate rock moulded into a god. Nothing more. Marble—metamorphosed calcium carbonate, with deep flaws and defects. If marble represented anything, it represented the face of death itself.

People around him knew Arjun Singh as a lovely young

bachelor—extremely unpopular in the marriage bazaar because of his opinionated views. His interest in science had something to do with it. Some people in the colony called him a frustrated scientist because he had failed to secure a regular position in his own specialization. He had ended up joining the Railways. The Railway Chief put him on the fast-track promotion scheme because of a degree in chemistry. Seven months ago the Chief had personally transferred Arjun Singh to the pesticide colony as the new stationmaster. Many freight trains stopped at the local station, and some were diverted all the way to the RATH Agri-Toxics and Chemicals Ltd.

Arjun Singh believed that the RATH factory was the *real temple* of India, gilded with modernity. RATH rinsed the brows of its devotees with the reality of ammonia, and not with dreams of an after-life. Chemicals provided heaven in this life. Irrigation canals and fertilizers, along with the molecules of pesticides, had ushered in the Green Revolution. The hiss of steam allowed a reunion with the memories of the conch shells in rock temples. The distillation columns were sculptures more erotic than the ones in ancient Khajuraho. In ornate pipelines flowed the answers to prayers of a billion souls.

Ten days after the miracle, Arjun Singh awoke at the usual hour, drank his glass of lassi, and pedalled a bicycle to the railway station. On the way he spotted the Saffron Politico's men zipping through the colony streets, riding motorized rickshaws. The rickshaws, dressed up, resembled the chariots in children's books of fairy tales and mythology. Shrill loudspeakers blared behind them.

One... a two... a three... test-ing... test-ing... MIKE test-ing... LOUDspeakkkurse test-ing.

Miracle-cle-cle-cle... Come one, come all... Come to widow apartment C-2/419... a one... a two... a three...test-ing.

"Superstitious people," thought Arjun Singh.

Visibly disturbed and distressed, he arrived at the station. But the same phenomenon awaited him there. He noticed unusual commotion. Trainloads of strange people poured out on the platforms. People from insalubrious slums and from skyscrapers. Beggars and professional people. Government clerks, poets, money-lenders, film stars, businessmen, prostitutes, policemen. Journalists from London. Even dogs—chasing the milk vendors. All eager to witness the site of the miracle. Eager to slither ahead of each other and offer milk to the widow's idol. Ganeshas the world-over were accepting milk, but only one idol belonged to the widow woman who had triggered the miracle. This was not some random chaos. The platforms were saturated with carnivalesque color. Even the billboards looked strange. The railway artists painted them with larger than life depictions of a woman in a white sari showering motherly love on baby Ganesha.

His day ended the way it started.

Arjun Singh found it hard to sleep that night despite a cold shower. Past midnight, he stepped out on the balcony and leaned on the iron railing. No one noticed him, perhaps only the strange birds, circling around the orange flames rising from the pesticide reactors and chimneys.

"Birds at this insane hour!" he said to himself. "Not one, not two, there are thousands, and they have blacked-out the chimneys."

Then a sari stirred on the neighbour's balcony. The widow's head was hooded by the pallu of her sari. She stood with hands folded in front of her. She seemed to be scanning the same smoke and flames. Behind her head glowed a giant halo, composed of pesticide dust. The halo partially blocked his view of the factory. He was about to protest when the woman turned her neck away from the strange birds and the pallu fell on her shoulders, and he noticed her hair tumbling down, and he appraised her figure—

absolute perfection in a white sari.

He mumbled inaudibly: "O unhappy creature, full of eloquent silence. Bliss assured to the one who caresses your pallu."

He watched Mrs. Chintamani, who, perhaps afraid of the silhouette on the adjacent balcony, retreated back into her room. Arjun Singh, still glued to the railing, once again caught sight of the strange birds. He arrived at a quick explanation: "The flames from the factory confuse the birds. The birds wake up in the middle of the night thinking these are the lights of the new dawn."

"One in a million. One in a million," he muttered praising the haloed woman. He knew that he stood no chance with her. He had probed her relative many times, but every time Vidya had repeated the same thing. "My cousin-sister thinks you are pompous and eccentric. You live inside clouds. You are just like the RATH factory, an atom bomb."

Next day Arjun Singh noticed a major anomaly at the station. The freight train—*Himalayan Queen*—pulled in twelve hours late. The delay was not unusual. The bizarre thing was that the freight train arrived with mountains of people—on its roof.

"That's odd," Arjun Singh said to his railway staff.

"Never in history, saar," said the gleeful deputies, "has our station scooped so many—"

"Attend to this matter," commanded the stationmaster. "Why did the train arrive with people instead of sulphur?"

"Saar, because of Shri-mat-i Chintamani."

"Front page news, saar. Papers published the lady photos, saar."

Numbers matter. Today 7.7 gallons of milk were sipped by the London Ganesha in 51.5 hours. Why? Because of our lady in the foothills of the Himalayas. When this correspondent questioned if this was her first miracle, the lady answered softly, "Ask trees, ask birds, ask the monsoon showers." (*The Times*).

"Ever met her?" asked the reverie-wrapped stationmaster as he slumped back in his chair.

"Saar," said the deputies, "the holy lady has large nimbus."

"It is smaller than it looks."

The freight train was carrying the notorious bandit, Chungapun, who had escaped the jungles of South India and was wanted by police for killing two thousand elephants and smuggling four million dollars worth of ivory.

The bandit had boarded the train to escape all the way to the mountains of Kashmir. But his plan had gone awry. From inside the stalled train he couldn't make head or tail of the frenzy on the platform. Nor could he comprehend the red-shirted porters, who were cursing the crowd. It was more an anarchy, less a crowd. Moneylenders, vegetable-wallahs, sadhus, French-Italian-German tourists, pimps, technicians, odissi dancers, clowns, drummers. For the first time in his life he was witnessing such an eclectic wave of passengers, dashing out of the train, without bags, carrying only hopes and prayers.

Chungapun, of course, knew nothing of prayer.

The night he was born, the amavasya night of the new moon, his mother died. His penniless father left the basket carrying the crying baby under a sandalwood tree and jumped into a deep river. Tiger lilies and elephants and local brigands had raised the boy. Childhood—that sprawling forest full of toys and fantasies— never took root within Chungapun. By eleven, the boy acquired the title of the regional gareeb-chor. At fourteen, haunted by the non-memories of his absent parents, he had reinvented himself as an ivory poacher. And now at fifty-four—despite dim eyes and somewhat damaged libido—his genius had achieved full recognition as 1,500 policemen worked around the clock for his arrest.

Chungapun twirled his long bushy moustache, tightened the red bandanna around his forehead, and descended from the train. Underneath his threadbare jacket he kept his beauty, a 0.315 Mauser, carefully concealed.

No one in the crowd noticed the darling of the newspapers. He descended the flight of stone stairs and landed in the street feeling like a businessman exploring opportunities in an alien city. Every step he took convinced him of his anonymity. He swelled his chest. People in this tiny town, he said to himself, must have suffered collective amnesia. The clock on the red tower across from the station moved twice as fast as the HMT watch on his wrist. While he squinted at the clock, he forgot the latest string of his crimes, which included the abduction of a veteran film star.

Chungapun asked the cabbie to follow the flux of pilgrims.

"Saar, cars not allowed at widow apartments!" replied the bare-chested man swerving his vintage 1948 Ambassador in the opposite direction.

"Arré, Go, Chaalo," demanded the passenger in Bollywood Hindi. His teeth glinted like daggers.

"Saar, only walking peoples allowed!"

"Baas… Bund bakwaas…" said the passenger. "This serves you right." He strangled the cabbie with his red bandanna. The dying man honked and honked, but to no avail. After disposing of the body, Chungapun fired up the engine and steered the cab slowly to the widow's alley.

The Saffron Politico, at that hour, was inside the widow's apartment keeping a count of the pilgrims and demanding money to build a big shrine at the site of the miracle. He ordered people to take off their shoes before entering the apartment. His assistants charged money for keeping an eye on the heaps of footwear which piled up outside. Bata shoes. Liberty sandals. Sona chappals.

Corona canvas boots. Duckback rubbers. The assistants hated those who arrived barefooted. They made the beggars wash their feet with potassium permanganate.

The Politico inspired a predatory zeal within people. He drugged them with words and explanations and he had solutions for everything.

Explanation for poverty: Muslims and Christian nuns and lesbians make India poor.

Solution for poverty: Remove Muslims to Pakistan and nuns to Albania and lesbians to Cuba.

Arjun Singh, that night between the hours of two and three, once again spotted the widow.

"Namasté," he said from his balcony.

"Namasté," she responded without hesitation from her balcony.

"You see, Mrs. C, I can't sleep a wink because of this miracle crowd of yours."

"Arjun ji, don't lie, please. Vidya has informed me already. I'm sorry that you suffer from bad insomnia."

"Madam, let us not quarrel. Who put the miracle idea in your head?"

"Arjun ji, miracle is not an idea, it is a feeling. One is graced. That is all."

"No, it's not what you feel. It's what you have been forced to feel by the Saffron Politico."

"Arjun ji, you are more suspicious than the married men. Namasté."

She slammed the door behind her. The song of the strange birds perched on the chimneys grew louder before it mingled with the shrieks of the real dawn. This only strengthened his resolve. Before dawn he slipped an audacious note under the Politico's tent:

I propose to test the miracle.

–Arjun Singh, B.Sc.

Two days later, Arjun Singh was summoned to the tent. On the way, fear and anxiety covered him with beads of sweat. He knew the Politico meant business. The man had not only threatened to demolish a precious 16th century monument, he had reduced it to rubble. He had burned 10,000 Muslims, Christians and 'Untouchables' in the name of building a Hindu Vatican. Now he was opposing a simple scientific demonstration. A test that was bound to open the eyes of superstitious people and contribute toward thrusting India into the twenty-first century. "There exist only two options for people like me," thought Arjun Singh. One: Live with fear. Two: Die for flame of reason.

"God has come down in this wicked age of Kali to remove afflictions of people and you plan to test Him," said the angry Politico. "No one tests Him."

"What you see is not true," said Arjun Singh. "And I can prove it."

"I shall only believe what I see," said the Politico.

"Science," said Arjun Singh, "is about things you don't see. Look at the structure of porous marble. Porous marble has capillary channels. When spoonful of milk is offered to the left tusk, the surface tension encourages the molecules of milk to be pulled in by molecules of marble."

"Where was this surface tension," protested the Politico, "for all those thousands of years when milk was offered to Ganesh-ji but he did not accept. Tell us why only now he drinks."

"He doesn't drink. But the marble does. And it does because, $\Delta P = -2\sigma\cos(\theta)/r$," said Arjun Singh while scribbling the equation on a piece of paper.

"God is not blotting paper."

"That is precisely what I mean."

"YOU ungrateful scum!"

"No need to raise voice JEE!"

Preparations for Arjun Singh's test were themselves a mini-miracle. Distinguished artists from Rajasthan were commissioned to sculpt a test-Ganesha, identical to the widow's Ganesha in every way except the material. Lunar-white blocks of non-porous marble were procured to construct the test-Ganesha. According to Arjun: The porous marble of widow's Ganesha would accept milk; and the non-porous marble of the test-Ganesha won't. Elementary!

The sculptors, while chipping away marble, praised Lord Ganesha extravagantly: *Marble the colour of mooncrest. Marble, sculpted into the compassionate elephant god, the one who adorns a snake band on his fat belly and rides a rat and wears loops of lightening as bangles. Ganesha, Shiva's mind-born celibate son, the one who holds in one of his hands the broken tusk—pointing downwards as if it were a pen. In other hands—lotus, pomegranate, parrot, fly-whisk. His eyes are dark and red and brown, always watching.*

On the amavasya night before Arjun Singh's test, a shadow, invisible to the guards, headed toward the two Ganeshas and bowed before the luminous marble formations. Delighted, he twirled his moustache. With the precision of a solid-state chemist, he began transferring the goods to the stolen Ambassador, parked by the factory chimneys. It was then that he heard the thunder. Dark, pesticide-laden clouds rolled above him and released their burden of rain. The rain smelled of boiled cabbage, wild onion, carrion spit. The bandit felt a burning sensation in his eyes. The widow's Ganesha, still in his hands, looked furious. Chungapun took it as a sign. He attempted to appease the offended god and stumbled back to the site of the crime.

He installed the twins back in the test room. Before leaving he examined them one last time, to make sure he had not damaged the goods. It seemed as if he had accidentally switched the gods, changed their positions. He struggled, switching the idols again and again, sniffing them again and again, until the coordinates matched the ones in his memory. Only then he ran towards Kashmir.

Arjun Singh, on that dark night, was shuffling nervously in his bed. He was contemplating the grand performance, only six hours away. Crowds always made him nervous. He brought to mind the words of a wise chemist-turned-writer, Elias Cannetti: *A crowd is the same as fire. Both spread rapidly. Both are contagious and insatiable. Both can break out anywhere. Both are destructive. Both have an enemy. Both die. Both act as if they were alive and are so treated.*

What calmed him ultimately was a cold shower and chapter six in the *Origin of Species*.

Next day, as the hour of the test approached, tension started building up at the widow's apartment. An unruly crowd of the National Milk Sellers' Union forced its way in through the backdoor entrance. Arjun Singh, wearing a brand new turban, had to squeeze in through hundreds of clerks and scientists and dancers and housewives and beggars who hummed around the test site. The perfume of rose petals, incense sticks, and vanished milk invaded his nostrils.

"Soon they'll witness the triumph of Reason over superstition," thought Arjun Singh.

A bevy of saffron thugs followed him with axes and other instruments of destruction. They had received strict instructions from the Politico: Kill Arjun if he falsifies the miracle. Otherwise, threaten to kill.

"Brothers and sisters! There is nothing supernatural about the missing milk," he began confidently.

—*Prove it!*

—*We'll burn you if you prove it!*

"Before I begin the demo, I would like to remind the anxious public of the purpose of the test."

From a sheet of typed paper, Arjun Singh (*B.Sc.*) read the following:

It shall be the duty of every citizen of India... to develop the scientific temper, humanism and the spirit of inquiry and reform.

—*Constitution of India* (Article 51-A(h))

—*Hurry!*

—*Hari!*

The chanting crowd pressed closer. So did the saffron-robed thugs. He instinctively knew that on his left was the non-porous Ganesha and on his right was the porous Ganesha. He looked straight at the widow, who stood between the two idols, her hands folded in front of her. She watched Arjun snapping nervously at a technician. She watched the teckie open a half-litre pack of pasteurized milk with scissors. She watched him empty the pack into a sterlized bowl.

Arjun Singh scooped up a spoonful from the bowl and quickly offered it to the tusk of the Ganesha on the left. Molecules of milk kneeled in prayer for a while but eventually they were wicked up. They were not supposed to be wicked up, murmured Arjun Singh. His breath quickened. He failed to notice Ganesha's gaze, the god's mildly astounded face.

When he offered milk to the Ganesha on the right, not a single drop was accepted.

The widow rang the bells.

The crowd chimed the spoons.

Outside, the milk vendors exploded fireworks.

The miracle was replicated.

That day his confidence was ruined forever, his science reduced to tatters, and he lost his grip on the world. He fell on his knees and kissed the blue hem of the divine woman's sari. Confronted with the unexplainable—his unique solitary religion shaken, fractured—he couldn't say all he wanted to say, so he wept. He was not alone. The people who flocked around him were like the strange birds he often observed from his balcony, the creatures that woke up early confused by the orange flames of pesticide. And it didn't matter if the "sun" was real or accidental, what mattered was the creation of some order within chaos.

The widow blushed and handed him the marble-white pallu of her muslin sari. His tears spread quickly inside the fine capillaries of the pallu, like dendrites, like sorrows of the world making way into an infinite sponge.

"This is how Prajapati, the Creator, wept," she pronounced softly, "seconds before inventing life and death."

The spectators looked at Arjun Singh with sympathy, while the Saffron thugs looked at him with fury. The Politico cracked a coconut.

"Now," spoke the widow in a transformed voice, "let no one hurt this man. From this day I will not only be concerned with my troubles only but with troubles of all of you."

"Jai Ganesh!" she said.

"*Jai Ganesh!*"

~

The Garden of Fidelity

Early morning, while picking cherries in the garden, Ms. Rubaiya Ghani Lone, sixty-three, thought of that distant Tuesday when her fast-friend called her mother ugly.

The day had not yet brightened in Kashmir, roosters not yet crowing. Two girls, as usual, were hurrying down the gravel path to school.

"Why your mother wears a veil?" asked Rekha.

"She likes it," replied Rubaiya.

"I know why."

"Tell me."

"Because she is ugly."

"No, she is not," said Rubaiya. "I am beautiful because my mother is beautiful."

"Let me tell you," said Rekha. "Your father, too, is ugly. But he hides his face with a henna-dyed beard. Do you know what that means?"

"What?"

"That your father and mother are not your *real* parents."

"They *are*," said Rubaiya. "And you are ugly."

"But, but, my parents are *really* my parents," said Rekha. "Also, my mother does not have a moustache."

Rubaiya's father, Abdul Ghani Lone, shivered when he saw his bold daughter sobbing outside the house. He had just returned from work in his blue shirt, pointed skullcap, and abundant beard. He worked as a foreman at the local watch factory, and knew all the springs of Time.

"Abba," she asked rubbing her tiny butterfly eyes, "why does Ammi wear a veil?"

"Now, now," he said, "on our wedding day your Ammi told me not to reveal the secret."

Seeing his daughter's brow disfigure, he changed the shape of his explanation. "Ammi is very beautiful, you see. Like an Empress. If she doesn't wear a veil, her beauty will explode like a bomb."

"Why then," she asked, "don't I wear a veil?"

"Arré," he said, "but first you must work hard. One is not born with the *thing*. One must labor to be beautiful."

Ghani Lone picked up the girl in his arms and transferred her indoors, then placed her on top of the three-legged table. Rubaiya's cat raised its tail on high, climbed the table and sailed past the basket of black cherries, towards the sobbing girl's thin legs.

"Look there at the mountains outside," he said, pointing his index finger towards the saggy window. "Always they look still, not moving, but every day they are growing. Every day they work hard to become beautiful. When these mountains were not there, millions of years ago, Kashmir was as ugly as Delhi."

From the kitchen Rubaiya's mother said, "Give her the real reason." Mother was cooking gushtaba, goat meatballs marinated in curd.

"Real reason," said Ghani Lone, "Ammi wears a veil is because she is God. She can see, but can't be seen."

Belkis Lone was a pragmatic woman with no patience for

fictions.

"Hold your tongue and do something useful," she said, rushing out of the smoky kitchen. She closed the front door of the house because Ghani Lone, as usual, had forgotten to do so. From the border a squad of fidayeen mosquitoes had dived in to occupy the space over her head.

During dinner she urged Ghani Lone to register a complaint with the headmistress. "Rekha was mean to our girl because her mother told her bakwas things about me. All because of that wretched competition."

The annual Womens' Musical Chairs competition was held on a Sunday, only two days before Rekha called Rubaiya's mother ugly. Chairs were set around a large cherry tree in the Garden of Fidelity. It was the only tree in the garden, planted in AD 1627 by Empress Noor Jahen herself.

Rekha's father, Mr. Kaul, moved seven chairs from his house that morning to the garden in a second-hand Ambassador car. Ghani Lone did not own a car, but he borrowed a brand-new musical machine from the watch factory and volunteered to play it impartially for the ladies.

The Indian army general's wife, as per the rules, acted as the judge for the competition. She made Ghani Lone sit on a rock by the tree, and instructed him not to look at the ladies while pressing the buttons of his machine—a chronometer, which mimicked the sound of roosters.

Mr. Kaul stood in the space between the tree and the circle of chairs around it. The chairs faced the audience, each person dressed in bright pherans, spilling colour like ripe apricots, plums, and juicy pears.

Each time Ghani Lone's music began, Mr. Kaul plucked a chair from the circle with great agility, so that there were exactly N-1 chairs for N ladies. Each time Ghani Lone's music paused, N-1 women sat down, and one of them walked out of the circle, accepting defeat gracefully.

Minutes before the decisive moment many in the audience leaped up on their feet. Only one chair left, and two ladies. Rekha's mother in her puff sleeved blouse and a chiffon sari, and Rubaiya's mother in her silken veil. Both equally determined to win the shahtoosh shawl, made of fibers so thin it was possible to pass the shawl through wedding rings. The competition was destined to end smoothly. Ghani Lone's roosters sounded as if they were slowly pecking away the seeds of uncertainty from sharp fingers of time.

It was then the children shouted. "The mule! The mule!"

The adults turned their necks, and noticed an artillery mule charging towards the garden. They were horrified. The mule had escaped the military stables the previous night and now without warning heading straight for the man on the rock.

Ghani Lone overreacted. He cranked up the roosters an octave higher, which disturbed the intruder like a lobbed grenade. Instead of behaving like a tamed animal, the mule did exactly the reverse. It trotted through the pink rhododendrons and for a minute stopped to examine the huge yellow magnolia. Then it leaped with red eyes over the open-mouthed spectators, landing close to the ladies by the tree, still competing.

The crowd, at once horrified and astonished by the mule's entry, its silver breath, and wild energy, froze into glacier-like immobility. Ghani Lone's music, too, froze. Thinking it was all over, he pivoted on the rock and was astonished to see his own wife perched on the solitary chair as if she was Empress Noor Jahen herself, alone in her garden. He made a V sign with his fingers and waited for the general's wife to pronounce Belkis Lone victorious.

Unfortunately, the defeated party, Mrs. Kaul, was lying on the ground, her chest moving up and down rapidly, her hairy legs exposed, for the entire world to see.

Generally she was a good loser, but that Sunday Mrs. Kaul rejected Belkis Lone's hand, the hand offered to her out of sheer generosity after the mule vanished from the lower terraces of the garden. Mrs. Kaul arose on her own, caught her breath, and protested that the animal had interfered in the competition.

"NO," said Belkis Lone. "The animal didn't interfere. And, if it did, both of us experienced it equally so."

Mrs. Kaul felt cheated. She banged her fist on the chair.

"No, it didn't interfere for you," she said, "because women in veils just can't see."

"In that case," said Belkis Lone, "you were just defeated by a blind woman."

The audience was stunned into silence. The general's wife sided with the Lones. It was then the Kauls loaded their Ambassador with all the seven chairs and left.

Belkis Lone refused to talk about the unpleasant incident with her family or friends in the garden, although her interior sizzled with anger. Her eyes welled up late in the evening when she accepted the fabled shawl from the general's wife. But the veil gave her face the public dignity it so badly needed. On the way home, Rubaiya waited for her mother's anger, but all she heard was a big zero.

Belkis Lone did speak her mind after the gushtaba dinner, and with all her accumulated anger.

"You are not playing with that Kaul girl again."

Wednesday, after school, the girls didn't talk to each other as they hurried back home. Their blue pherans fluttered like flags on the gravel path. On the left side of the path were the blasted orchards, and on the right side was the fence. The path ran parallel to the border between India and Pakistan, mined at places, and patrolled by men in full battle-dress. Brightly painted military trucks crawled on both sides, as if by pure inertia. From the soil bloomed concrete posts and cast-iron shrubbery, infested with orange rust. "The military protects the maps in your atlas," Rubaiya's father had told her not long ago.

Not talking was good, thought Rubaiya, because Rekha didn't get to issue big lies this way. Although she felt ill at ease with the silence, Rubaiya was happy they were only a few yards away from home. The cat came prowling towards her, tail on high. Rubaiya picked up the creature, and ran towards the roosters in front of the house. Rekha followed stealthily.

"Don't follow," said Rubaiya, crossing her eyes. "My mother will explode you with the bomb of her beauty. She is more beautiful than the Empress."

Rekha contorted her pencil-thin nose, still chasing Rubaiya. "Come on," she said, "The cat is beautiful, but it does not wear a veil. You are beautiful, but you don't wear a veil. You know what this means?"

"What?"

"The cat is your *real* mother."

Rubaiya, consumed by anger, picked up a pebble outside the house and aimed at Rekha, missing her by a few millimetres, hitting the rooster instead. The bird fluttered in pain. As the bird settled high on the roof, the cat slipped out of Rubaiya's arms.

"Indira! Indira!" Rubaiya yelled, at the top of her voice.

The cat cut through the road used by the Shaktiman military trucks and leaped over the 'Do Not Speed Over My Curves' sign. Rubaiya ran after the cat. Rekha chased them with a sharp pebble. Indira was about to cross the border when the forest of soldiers on both sides of the barbed wire became jumpy.

Fire!

Fire!

Rubaiya and Rekha trembled, but they did exactly what their parents had told them to do during shelling at the border. Both crawled under a muddy military truck and put fingers in ears. Afraid, they felt like hugging each other, but sat far apart, not exchanging a word. A few drops of diesel leaked on their ponytails as the girls tried monitoring Indira's movements.

By the time the firing stopped, dusk had descended in the valley. A mauve cloth of light hung on the Indian side of the border. A jungle of boots marched up and down, looking for the intruder. Still under the truck, the girls heard a roar of the motor. Both flattened themselves to the ground, pretending to be dead. But, the motor was silent again, and the truck didn't roll. Only the exhaust fumes rolled away.

Rekha, her face smeared with grease, hunched up a little and dug both hands in the pockets of her pheran. She discovered her mother's forbidden lipstick there, and reddened her lips bright.

"Don't cry," she said to Rubaiya. "If I give you the lipstick your so-called mother will beat you."

Rubaiya cried louder, her small fists penetrating both eyes.

"My cat is dead!"

"Not true," said Rekha, pointing her finger towards the military truck on the other side of the border.

Indira was stretching its hind legs under a Pakistani truck. Its tail was painted with blood. She looked dizzy. Her eyes were pools of green—swelling now shrinking now, mimicking wide waves in the lake hidden under the Tiger Mountain. The truck backed up a little, turned, and squealed as it hit the road. The cat dashed towards a dangling metal chain, grasped it at the rear, and sailed away.

"Now why are you crying?"

"She is not with me."

"You know what this means," said Rekha.

"What?"

"You are a Pakistani spy."

"I am a Kashmiri."

"All the same," said Rekha. "Your mother lives on the other side of the border."

Rubaiya wept like monsoon rain. Monsoon never makes it to Kashmir, but the girls had seen its glint in Bombay films. Rekha tried her best to calm her ex-friend, she even gave her lipstick.

"Don't cry," she said. "They will take care of Indira."

"Only I can take care of my cat."

"You can't even take care of your su-su."

Rubaiya noticed a long brownish line of liquid tagged to her muddy boots, ending in a puddle. It was less a line, more a spiral, some strange geometry, but with a familiar smell. She felt both warm and cold inside.

"I told you so," said Belkis Lone. "Stay away from that Kaul girl."

Rubaiya found her mother sitting on the carpet, embroidering. In the dim light of a kerosene lamp, she was embroidering new pherans, embedding arabesques in them. The flame was getting dimmer and dimmer but that was all right. Because of shelling at the border the entire town was under a blackout.

Belkis Lone, all that day, she had sat behind the USHA sewing machine, the one with rusty crank handle, and she stitched pherans for Rubaiya, as if she well knew the state in which her daughter would return that night—burdened by grease and stink and black metal, every single strand of cloth ripped apart by a rabid dog.

Rubaiya, all that night, felt pain in her ears; she couldn't sleep at all. Tiny eyes kept surveying her mother's bony, mysterious face.

She kept listening to her mother's spidery threads and needles, and when that stopped, she listened to the rocks tumbling down from high mountains. The mountains, she thought, were in pain, too, just like her, shedding big, solid tears.

She was sure her mother was hiding things from her. Suspicions grew when Belkis Lone announced that she had made two pherans instead of one.

"Who is the other one for? For your *real* daughter?" she asked.

"You are my *real* daughter," said Belkis Lone. "Is this what I get for laboring so hard? Tell me?"

Ghani Lone, half-awake, muttered from his bed, "Both pherans are for you only. If you keep rummaging like chickens under military trucks you will need a pheran a month, no? Keep an extra in your bag—for emergency situations only."

The girl sulked in her bed, hands clung tightly to the pillow.

"Not your *real* mother," said Belkis Lone extinguishing the lamp. "Even if that Kaul girl tells you the same bakwas a hundred more times, you will remain my daughter."

Thursday, before he left for the factory, Ghani Lone switched on his clock-transistor and turned the dial to Radio Kashmir. He could not believe his ears.

"The end of the world," he announced, "has been postponed."

On the radio they kept repeating that after twenty-four years, nine months, and six days, the gates were finally going to open. The Indian and Pakistani generals were going to shake hands at the border.

The news made him forget the previous night's shelling and sent a wave of hope within his tired body, and for once he started conjuring up a new world, a world in which he could synchronize all the old watches in his collection.

Belkis Lone was not so hopeful. She dismissed the news as a

new stunt by the politicians. She accompanied her daughter to school to register a complaint with the headmistress about Rekha's mean behavior. People were rushing up and down the gravel path, carrying their shadows. A woman's bangle got caught in her veil, and as Belkis Lone was trying to pull it free, a few strands came off the silken cuff.

The headmistress looked frazzled.

"No time for complaints," she said to the mother.

"And you, Rubaiya," said the headmistress, "LINE UP."

"Right away, madam?"

"We don't have much time," she said.

Out in the dusty compound, the Indian general's camouflaged car was parked, and a few soldiers were leaning against it. The general was inside the assembly hall, inspecting the girls as if they were new recruits in his regiment.

"Today," he boomed, "we need a girl to accompany us."

The girls whispered.

"Silence," said the headmistress. "Pin-drop silence."

The general was a tall man with a clipped gray beard and sparkling shoulders. His chest was loaded with medals. He wore a gold watch and gold-rimmed glasses, which were unable to hide icy eyes. Rubaiya saw her face reflected in his neatly polished black boots. His leather belt had a silver front, and it was so wide she could walk on the thing without fear of falling.

"This one," said the general to the headmistress, pointing towards the last girl in the line.

"I like the arabesques on her pheran. This one will come with us."

"I too," cried the girl standing in the middle of the line.

"Girl," said the general, looking over his shoulder. "What did you say?"

"I too," said Rekha.

The headmistress put a finger on her lips and stared at Rekha. The general marched towards the girl. His boots screeched the wooden floor as he marched.

"Next time beauty-cutie," he said. "Next time we will take you to Pakistan."

"Now," cried Rekha. "Now."

Rubaiya felt for her mean ex-friend. Really she wanted the whole class to accompany her to Pakistan to bring Indira home, but she quickly decided against the idea.

"General sir," she said, "In the bag that my Ammi is holding I have another pheran. Same to same. Can we take one more girl along?"

The general winked his icy eye.

She ran to her mother and without permission dug out the pheran from the bag. Then she ran to Rekha and said, "That woman over there in a veil stitched this thing. Do you know what this means?"

"She must be your mother."

The general drove the girls to the border. A huge crowd of on-lookers had gathered there as if they were all pilgrims in a procession. The cast iron gates were still locked. Through the bars a thick white line on the tarred road was visible. *Kashmir is the rose in our bouquet*—announced a dirty sign on the Indian side. *Kashmir is the heart of our nation*—announced an equally dirty sign on the Pakistani side.

Minutes after the general disembarked from the camouflaged car, the Indian and Pakistani guards raised the national flags of their respective countries, accompanied by bugles. The wind was so strong on that Thursday, it maddened the flags, tossing them this way and that. Mountain division army bands, on both sides, played bagpipes and snare-drums.

The crowd whistled when the Indian general entered Pakistan to shake hands with his counterpart. Hundreds applauded furiously when two hesitant girls stepped across the line, and more so when Rekha and Rubaiya floated on their toes and handed flowers to the Pakistani general. Roses. Tulips. Pelargoniums.

The enemy general, his khaki breast loaded with medals, bent down and patted the girls on their backs, while the acrobatic photographers took pictures.

Belkis Lone and Mrs. Kaul could not hold back their tears when they witnessed the girls create a bridge of peace. Both stood in the pavilion with lifted hands, waving. But when the bandmaster and his boys marched back to the front row, the view was blocked. Seeing an empty chair not far from the army officers' wives row, Belkis Lone ran full tilt towards it. But, she stopped midway when she noticed that a determined Mrs. Kaul was heading for the same chair. Mrs. Kaul stopped, too, the moment she felt the presence of her rival. In that mobile-immobile confusion they lost the chair to a man with a thick moustache and arrogant whiskers. The women stood behind the occupied chair. Together they watched their daughters cross the border, beyond the blasted trees, and for one brief moment they turned and surveyed each other. During that moment they didn't have the courage to hold each other's hands—their fingers twitched—but certainly both of them felt that it was not too late, perhaps, to immerse themselves, once again, in a mild, but beautiful, friendship.

~

Heaven

In Kashmir, near Kargil, there was an old man who knew how to climb the tallest mountain and become lighter than air. To keep alive he ate snow, and when people asked him why he ate snow, he answered, "It is not forbidden."

Always a trail of children formed behind him.

Once the boy Adi asked, "Baba, why do you keep climbing the same mountain again and again?"

"Boy," he answered, "I am calculating the distance to heaven."

Time passed. The man correctly and satisfactorily calculated the distance. Yet he never stopped trudging up the slopes of the mountain. He had grown very old and the boy had turned into a tall man.

"Baba," Adi asked him one day with a smile, "now, why do you keep climbing? Isn't it boring?"

"The distance to heaven," the old man replied with a whiff of sadness, "is not a constant, as I thought earlier. It fluctuates with the population of the birds."

"This means," the boy interpreted, "you will never be successful."

The old man fell on his knees, smiled, and scooped up some freshly fallen snow from the trail. As he began eating the flakes one by one he turned to the boy and said, "All it means is that more work is required."

Acknowledgements

Thanks to Mark Jarman, for introducing my work to Canadian readers, and for being the first to suggest that I expand my two stories into a book; to Tamara Straus, the editor of *Zoetrope*, for publishing the title story; to Andrew Steinmetz, fiction editor at Véhicule Press, for his 'pitiless eye and a worrying heart'; Simon Dardick and his wonderful team at Véhicule—Scott McRae, Vicki Marcok; and Denise Bukowski, my agent.

Thanks to everyone involved with the Summer 2002 Writing Studio at the Banff Centre for the Arts; and to the Canada Council for the Arts, for providing time to work on the book.

For known and unknown reasons I would like to thank Arvinder Singh, Avneet Vohra, Elizabeth Hay, Fred Stenson, Lissa Cowan, Marjan Radjavi, Nidhi Srinivas, Rina Bansal, Rosa Sundar-Maccagno, Sharmila Rudrappa, Tanya Handa, Trevor Ferguson, Umarraj Saberwal, and Yumna Siddiqi. Many thanks to all my friends from whom I received comments on work-in-progress and words of encouragement. I am deeply indebted to a long list of short story writers, both living and dead. Special thanks to Subrata Mandal, organizer of the Montreal Cricket League, for providing cricket balls to designer David Drummond who created a splendid cover—no sari, no veil, no spice, no gun.

'Captain Faiz' relied on anecdotes from the India-Pakistan wars and WW1; 'Remover of Obstacles' relied on news reports obtained from nine international papers. 'Angle of Heaven' was inspired by a conversation with Dr. Parvez Hoodbhoy. 'The Garden of Fidelity' was inspired by a BBC broadcast of Peter Sheridan's *Freckles*, and by W.B. Yeats' *Adam's Curse*.

Excerpts from the Los Bravos song: "Black is Black," appear on pages 90 and 95. "Arjun" appeared earlier in *The Fiddlehead* under a different title, "Kanak" (Summer 2001). "Seventeen Tomatoes" appeared in *Zoetrope* (Winter 2002).

Jaspreet Singh

ESPLANADE
Books

THE FICTION SERIES AT VÉHICULE PRESS

[Series Editor: Andrew Steinmetz]

A House by the Sea
A novel by Sikeena Karmali

A Short Journey by Car
Stories by Liam Durcan

Seventeen Tomatoes: Tales from Kashmir
Stories by Jaspreet Singh

Véhicule Press
www.vehiculepress.com